Ticktock, ticktock . . .

Frank read the plane ti[...] seven a.m. flight tomor[...] five o'clock that night. N[...]

"I guess if we don't find the bomb and the bad guys, we're useless," I said.

Just then, Mom knocked on the door.

I closed the video game player and called, "Come on in."

Mom poked her head inside and looked at us suspiciously. "I was walking by your door when I heard something strange."

Uh-oh. I looked to Frank, who quickly hid the plane tickets between the mattress and box spring of his bed.

THE HARDY BOYS

UNDERCOVER BROTHERS™

Available from Simon & Schuster

THE HARDY BOYS

UNDERCOVER BROTHERS

#10 **Blown Away**

FRANKLIN W. DIXON

Aladdin Paperbacks

New York   London   Toronto   Sydney

This book is a work of fiction. Any references to historical events, real people, or real locales are used fictitiously. Other names, characters, places, and incidents are the product of the author's imagination, and any resemblance to actual events or locales or persons, living or dead, is entirely coincidental.

❦ ALADDIN PAPERBACKS
An imprint of Simon & Schuster
Children's Publishing Division
1230 Avenue of the Americas
New York, NY 10020

Copyright © 2006 by Simon & Schuster, Inc.

THE HARDY BOYS MYSTERY STORIES and HARDY BOYS UNDER-COVER BROTHERS are trademarks of Simon & Schuster, Inc.
ALADDIN PAPERBACKS and colophon are trademarks of Simon & Schuster, Inc.
Designed by Lisa Vega
The text of this book was set in Aldine 401BT.
Manufactured in the United States of America
First Aladdin Paperbacks edition June 2006
20 19 18 17 16 15 14 13 12 11

Library of Congress Control Number 2005931824
ISBN-13: 978-1-4169-1173-9
ISBN-10: 1-4169-1173-1
0412 OFF

TABLE OF CONTENTS

Blown Away

1

Shredding

No way am I gonna survive this.

That's what I was thinking as I tore down the icy slope, at what had to be a ninety-degree angle. There was nothing between me and the mountain but a thin fiberglass snowboard. One mistake, one rock or slick spot or bad turn, and I'd be history.

What a rush.

Of course, it didn't matter that my adrenaline was pumping. This wasn't about fun. Frank and I had a big problem: Regardless of how fast we shredded down the mountain, Chaz and Brad were faster. It made sense, since they were pro snowboarders—or pro snowboarders turned drug dealers, to be more exact. But that didn't mean Frank and I weren't gonna catch them.

This was our latest ATAC mission. We'd successfully targeted the bad guys, staked 'em out, and gathered all the evidence. Their meticulous record of drug deals as well as their latest stash were both secured in the inner pocket of my snowboard jacket. Problem was, the bad guys were getting away.

The chase began twenty minutes after the lifts stopped running, so other than the four of us, the mountain was deserted.

Just as we started making progress, Chaz and Brad took a detour. They were leading us down Doomed River Run, which had been closed all season because of avalanche threats.

"They think we're not gonna follow them," I called to Frank. "Like a few skull-and-crossbones danger signs would ever stop us!"

"Yeah, they thought wrong," Frank replied, as he took a sharp left and barreled past another warning sign.

In the distance I saw the guys in front of us crouch down, and then soar into the air. We were coming up on a jump. "Get ready," I warned Frank.

"I'm always ready," my brother replied.

I got into position, holding the edge of my board with one gloved hand.

Then I went for it. Suddenly I was flying through the air—weightless and graceful like an eagle. It was awesome. And before I could even blink, I made a smooth landing, pointing the left side of my board straight down the mountain. I had to pick up speed—otherwise, these crooks would get away.

When we hit the next clearing, the guys disappeared. Not good. If they made it to the bottom of the mountain they'd be able to blend in with the crowd and eventually flee. Plus, the sun was setting, and finding them in the dark would be impossible.

There had to be another way.

Just then I saw it. *Zip line*—the two words came to me in a flash of genius. Above our heads was an empty steel cable, linking the top of the mountain to the bottom in a clean, straight line. It must have been part of an old ski lift. There weren't any chairs or gondolas attached, as far as I could tell. Using it as a zip line would get me to the bottom of the mountain in no time. I yelled my plan to Frank.

"You're crazy!" he said.

"Says you," I replied, as I skidded to a stop and ditched my board. I pulled my scarf from my neck. I was sure the fleece and wool blend would be strong enough to hold me. Well, pretty sure. Working for ATAC, I've jumped out of planes with broken parachutes, survived explosions and roaring fires, scuba dived to dangerous depths and more. What's one more risk?

By now Brad and Chaz were two specks in the distance, and even Frank was fading from my view. I had to act fast. I scrambled up the pine tree closest to the steel cable. When I was high enough, I jumped.

Bingo. I was on, hanging literally by a thread. My legs dangled down, swaying with the wind. I slung one end of my scarf around the cable and held on tight. Then I pushed off, shifting the bulk of my weight forward.

Woo-hoo! I was really flying.

Trees whipped by so fast that all I saw was a blur of green. A steady rain was falling, but at my speed, the drops felt more like an assault. They stung every part of my face that wasn't covered by my mask or helmet.

I shot past Frank, and soon, past Chaz and Brad. It was awesome. At least, that's what I was thinking until I spotted the gondola at the end of the line.

Brakes. Why didn't I think about brakes?!

Too late. I was about three seconds from crashing. I'd broken bones before, but never all of 'em at once. . . .

I glanced down at the thirty-foot drop. Too bad for me. I had no other choice.

I let go and fell, too scared to even gasp.

My stomach shot up to my throat. And then, all I saw was white.

I felt no pain, only cold. That was good. The powder broke my fall.

Of course, the powder also buried me.

First thing I did was carve out an air pocket in the snow so I could take a deep breath. Then I raised my hands above my head and started digging. I scrambled out as quickly as I could, pushing past the snow furiously. You'd think that powder would be light, but let me tell you—when it's packed into a ten-foot pile that's been sitting around since last week's snowfall, it's not. The powder was heavy. Very heavy. When I finally crawled to the surface my arms were sore and I was gasping for breath. Still, I bolted to the base of the run.

On my way there I pulled my cell phone from my pocket and dialed Chief Chizzle, the head of the Lake Tahoe police department. "We got 'em at the bottom of the mountain—south side, at the end of the Doomed River Run. Yeah, I know it's closed. It wasn't my idea. Anyway, their ETA is about forty-five seconds. Better get a move on."

When I reached the base, Chaz and Brad were on their butts, unlocking their feet from their boards. I got there just in time—to get whacked in the face with Brad's snowboard.

Oh, man, that hurt. Doubling over, I tried to catch my breath. My brain felt like it was exploding. My eyes were tearing, and I seriously saw stars. But there wasn't time for pain. I couldn't let those sleazebags get away. I stood up, my whole body aching.

I was still recovering when Frank came down the mountain, full speed ahead, and crashed right into Chaz and Brad. They went down like bowling pins.

As Frank took off his board, the guys got up, but I managed to stall them with a quick right hook to Chaz's chin and a fake, then a one-two punch in Brad's fleshy gut.

The guys were still on the ground when the cops showed.

"Good work, boys," said Chief Chizzle.

A couple of his officers hauled Brad and Chaz to their feet so they could slap on the handcuffs.

"We'll get you for this," Brad yelled.

"You're gonna have to wait about thirty years," I replied. "And that's only if you get out of jail early, for good behavior."

Chaz tried to lunge for me but the cops restrained him.

"Come on, Joe," my brother said. "It's over now."

"Hey, he started it," I argued, nodding my chin toward Chaz.

"He's already in handcuffs," Frank said. "We're done here."

"Fine," I said. Turning to Chief Chizzle, I handed over the envelope. "All of your evidence is in here."

As the chief looked through the contents, he said, "Well done, boys. Please send my best to your father."

"Will do," said Frank, with a quick salute to the chief. "Speaking of . . . Hey, Joe, what time is it?"

I checked my watch. "Almost seven o'clock."

"Uh-oh." Frank's face went pale.

I knew exactly what he was thinking.

We both took off at a sprint. Surviving Doomed River Run and delivering a couple of sleazy drug dealers to the cops was nothing compared to our new problem: If we were late for dinner, our mom was gonna kill us.

2

The Visitor

Mom noticed how busted up we were as soon as we walked through the cabin's front door. She dropped her book, got off the couch, and rushed over to Joe, crying, "Honey, what happened?"

Whoops—we'd been in such a hurry, we'd forgotten to come up with an excuse to explain why half of Joe's face looked like raw hamburger meat.

"Nothing," said my brother, as he held his hand up to his cheek and winced. "Uh, I wiped out, is all. No big deal."

"Come on. Don't downplay it." I turned to our mom and explained. "You know Joe. He was showing off, trying to do an 'Air to Fakie' off this steep jump, and then bam!" I clapped my hands together.

"He came down at some crazy angle and fell flat on his face, in front of about thirty people."

Joe glared at me and I shrugged. Hey, I had to come up with a believable cover, right? My brother hamming it up for a crowd—that was a no-brainer.

Mom headed to the freezer and started filling a plastic bag with ice. "Oh, Joe. I wish you'd be more careful," she said. "You were at least wearing a helmet, right?"

"Yes, Mom."

"You know that five to ten percent of all ski injuries involve the head. And that injuries to the head are the most lethal of all, and that—"

"And that wearing a helmet significantly reduces the chance of a fatality," Joe finished. "Yup, I know the stats."

Having a reference librarian for a mother sure keeps us on our toes.

Mom handed Joe the ice pack. "If the swelling doesn't go down in a couple of hours, I'm taking you to a doctor."

"I'll be fine," Joe insisted. "It doesn't even hurt."

As he raised the ice to his face, he cringed. Seeing him in pain made me wish I'd hit those sleazebags harder.

A minute later Dad came home from his afternoon of cross-country skiing. When he saw Joe, his face registered concern, but not surprise. "Come over here, son. Let's take a look at that gash in the light."

Joe walked over and Dad tilted his chin up and squinted at the bruise. "How much does it hurt?"

"Hardly at all. It was just a little wipeout," said Joe. "I'll be fine."

No need to embellish with Dad. He knew all about our mission. Dad is the founder of ATAC, American Teens Against Crime. Even though he's retired, he's still clued in as to what's going on. In fact, Dad planned our family vacation at the last minute, around the snowboarding drug dealers' bust. He said it was just a fluke that our spring break happened to coincide with the mission, and that he's been wanting to take us to Lake Tahoe for years. *As if!* We figure Dad knew that Chaz and Brad were hard-core criminals. He was probably so worried about us, he jumped at any excuse to be nearby.

Not that I'm complaining. It was great to be on a family vacation. Aunt Trudy isn't much of a skier, so she'd stayed home in Bayport to take care of Playback, our pet parrot. It was just me, Joe, Mom and Dad, and the mountains. Lake Tahoe was awesome, and ski conditions were amazing.

After four days of pursuing criminals, I was

stoked to take a break. Snowboarding for fun would be great. We hadn't even been to the back bowls yet. And maybe we'd hit Doomed River Run again. Sure it was closed, but it hadn't seemed *that* dangerous. . . .

At least that's what I was thinking when I heard a knock on the door.

Mom and Dad were in the kitchen finishing up dinner, and Joe was lying on the couch with the ice pack on his face, so I went to answer it.

"Uh, hi," I said, opening the door. Brilliant, I know. But seeing this totally cute girl on the doorstep was a shock. She was on the short side, with dark skin and large brown eyes. Her curly black hair was pulled up in a ponytail, and she was wearing the cutest pink snowsuit. My hands got sweaty and my tongue seemed to swell. Even if I'd had a clue about what to say, I didn't think I'd be able to spit it out.

Luckily, she wasn't waiting. "I'm looking for Joe Hardy," she said.

Phew.

"Right here," said Joe, coming up right behind me. "Can I help you with something?"

"I don't think so," said the girl. "But I can help you."

"Huh?" asked Joe.

"I'm Cammie," she said, handing Joe a snowboard. "And I believe that this is yours."

"My snowboard," said Joe. "I left it by the zip line and I totally spaced. How did you know where to find me?"

"Your name is on the board," said Cammie.

"No, it's not," said Joe, with this completely confused expression on his face. "It's a rental."

Cammie punched his arm and winked. "I said your name is on the board," she repeated, in an urgent whisper.

"Huh?" asked Joe.

I cut in, whispering, "You're with ATAC?"

She nodded.

"It's okay. Our mom and dad are in the kitchen. They can't hear us," Joe said.

"Okay, good deal," said Cammie. "Great work with Chaz and Brad, guys. I'm impressed."

I felt my cheeks heat up. "Um . . ."

"Thanks," said Joe. "What are you doing later on? Maybe we can meet up tomorrow afternoon and I'll tell you all about it. Do you ice skate?"

Joe isn't one to beat around the bush. Especially with girls.

Cammie laughed. "I won't be meeting you tomorrow."

Dissed, I thought. I clapped my brother on the back and said, "Nice try, guy."

"Okay," said Joe, shrugging me off. "It's cool. It doesn't have to be ice-skating, if you don't want. We can go bowling, or just grab a bite to eat."

Cammie shook her head. "I love ice-skating, but you're really not getting it. You're not going to be here tomorrow."

"I'm not?" asked Joe.

Sometimes my brother can be slow. I whipped the board around. Taped to the back of it was a large padded envelope. "Check it out, Joe."

"Aha!" he said, leaning against the doorframe and crossing his arms over his chest. "I get it. Otherwise, you'd be happy to go out with me, right?"

"Boys," Mom called from the kitchen. "Dinner is ready!"

Cammie laughed. "Sounds like you've got to go."

As she walked away, Joe called, "Okay, but would you have gone?"

Cammie looked over her shoulder and winked. "That's for me to know and for you to always wonder about."

"Harsh," said Joe.

Meanwhile, I ripped the envelope off the snowboard and opened it up. Inside was a disc labeled BLOWN AWAY, two passes for an antique car show, a map of a resort, and a couple of plane tickets.

Looked like we were about to take a little vacation from our vacation. . . .

JOE

3

Operation Blown Away

I was dying to know what our latest mission was, but we didn't have time to play the disc just then because we had to eat.

Then, after dinner, Mom asked, "Who's up for a game of Scrabble?"

Uh-oh. I looked at Frank, who just shrugged.

Thanks for coming up with an out, dude.

Not.

I cleared my throat. "Um, actually, Mom, Frank and I were planning on playing some video games."

Mom looked totally crushed. "You brought your portable game player on our family vacation?" she asked.

"Sort of," I had to admit. "Dad did just get it for me for my birthday. I figured it would have been rude not to take it, you know?"

Mom wasn't buying it. "It's bad enough that you boys switched to snowboarding, so we can't even ski together as a family anymore. Now you want to lock yourselves in a small bedroom to stare at the television?"

"Oh, don't worry. It's not the TV," I said. "The game player has its own screen."

My brother kicked me. Frank turned to her and said, "I think you're forgetting that the game is educational."

Mom raised her eyebrows and asked, "Oh really, Frank. How do you figure that?"

"It allows us to practice hand-eye coordination," he replied.

That's my bro!

"Maybe on toddlers," said Mom.

"Frank's not that mature," I piped in.

He kicked me again, but this time I got him back.

"Ow," he said.

I grinned and wiggled my eyebrows. "Something wrong, Frank?"

"No," he grumbled.

Mom wasn't gonna give up. "Now, boys, are you forgetting that we're in Lake Tahoe? Just look out the window. There are gorgeous mountains right outside."

"And you want us to stay cooped up here so we can play a board game?" I asked.

"We've been outside all day, Mom," said Frank. "Look at what the outside did to Joe's face. Come on. Give us a break."

Dad started laughing.

"What's so funny?" Mom and Frank asked at the same time.

"You're never going to win this argument," Dad said, as he stood up and began clearing the table. "Just accept the facts."

"Are you talking to us or to Mom?" I wondered.

"Hmm," said Dad. "You know what? Forget I said anything. I think I'm better off not taking sides."

"I have an idea," said Mom. She turned to Frank and me. "How about if you boys play your video game for an hour, and after that, we can play Scrabble as a family."

"Deal," I said. And then we bolted upstairs.

The cabin Mom and Dad had rented for us had just two bedrooms, so Frank and I were sharing for the week. He made sure our door was shut tight, and I headed straight to the portable game player.

As I popped in the disc and hit play, we both

huddled over the screen in anticipation. We knew the drill by now. All of our ATAC missions came to us via video game discs.

This time, some elevator music started blaring from the speakers. Blech. I could totally live without that. Then the screen blinked and an image of some fancy hotel in the middle of the desert came on. Soon we heard the deep voice of some guy with a British accent. It didn't sound like Q, the agent who usually spoke on these CDs—maybe it was one of the other guys on his team.

"Located just outside of Phoenix, Arizona, the Billington Resort and Spa is one of the finest hotels in the country. Every president since Theodore Roosevelt has vacationed there. And today, the resort is a popular destination for celebrities and world leaders. In fact, it was just bought by Jake Beller, the real estate mogul and reality television star."

"Cool," I said. I knew all about Jake Beller. His show was called *The Candidate*. He recruited people from all over the country and they competed, on camera, for a job running one of his companies. "That guy owns everything. And isn't he about to marry that model/actress? What's her name? Emma, or Eddy, or someone?"

"Shh," said Frank.

My brother is so serious.

The British voice droned on. *"This weekend the resort is hosting two high-profile events."* Just then an image of Beller and the model/actress flashed on the screen. *"The first is Jake Beller's wedding to Ella Sinclair. They are expecting more than three hundred guests, and they will spend an estimated million dollars on the party."*

"A million dollars on one wedding!" I exclaimed. "That's insane."

"Jake Beller is one of the richest men in America," Frank pointed out.

"Still . . ."

The image changed from Beller and Ella Sinclair to some of the coolest old sports cars I'd ever seen.

"And number two," said the voice, *"is the M&P Car Auction, the biggest annual antique car auction in the world. There are one hundred forty-five vintage cars on view, worth a total of more than fifteen million dollars."*

Fifteen million bucks on a bunch of cool cars? *That* I have no problem with. "This is gonna be so excellent. I wonder what the problem is," I said.

It was like the mysterious British guy was listening in on our conversation. *"The problem is,"* he said, *"ATAC recently found out that there's a bomb somewhere on the premises. It's powerful enough to blow up the entire resort—along with everyone and everything in it. The bomb is set to go off at three o'clock tomorrow afternoon. If* the bomb goes off, everything—and everyone—will be blown to bits. It will destroy the property. It may cost lives, do tens of millions of dollars in damage, and send a bad message to the terrorists.

"Besides identifying and detaining the guilty party, you'll need to find the bomb and contact the bomb squad—they'll be standing by and ready to defuse it. If you don't find the bomb by two o'clock, the resort will have to be evacuated so no one gets injured. Evacuation is a last resort."

"Doesn't sound too complicated," Frank said.

It didn't, but seeing the simulated explosion, even in cartoonlike graphics, gave me the heebie-jeebies. The screen filled up with smoke.

"Complications will arise," said the voice. "Neither Jake Beller nor Henry Peterson, the owner of the M&P Car Auction, will cooperate with the authorities. The two men have a history of conflict. Neither man wanted to share the resort this weekend. Each wanted the other to switch dates, but both refused. This made them very unhappy. Both are used to getting what they want. Jake tried to bribe Henry and when that didn't work, he threatened to sue. Henry didn't like that. Each has threatened the other, and they've both hired their own security forces for the weekend. It's a mess—too complicated for our adult secret agents. But you boys should be *able to sneak in under the radar. As always, you must be careful to stay undercover. If either party finds out who you are, they'll throw you out."*

"What kind of jerks won't even cooperate with the police?" I asked.

"The kind of jerks who have something to hide," Frank replied.

"You will leave first thing tomorrow morning. This mission, like every mission, is top secret," said the voice. *"In five seconds this disc will be reformatted into a regular music CD."*

As promised, five seconds later the game player started blasting the elevator music. I switched it off.

Frank read the plane tickets. "We need to catch a seven a.m. flight tomorrow, and we come home at five o'clock that night. Not much time."

"I guess if we don't find the bomb and the bad guys, we're useless," I said.

Just then, Mom knocked on the door.

I closed the video game player and called, "Come on in."

Mom poked her head inside and looked at us suspiciously. "I was walking by your door when I heard something strange."

Uh-oh. I looked to Frank, who quickly hid the

plane tickets between the mattress and box spring of his bed.

"It sounded like Beethoven's Fifth," Mom continued. "Are you boys listening to classical music?"

Phew. She really had me there for a second. "We sure were," I said.

"Really?" she asked.

I nodded. "Yes, we can only take so much rap, hip hop, and ska. Classical music is so . . . classic."

Mom placed her hands on her hips and smiled. "This is such a nice surprise," she said.

We both grinned back at her. What else were we going to do?

"You know, Mom," said Frank. "I've been thinking about what you said, and you're totally right. We hardly ever spend family time together. The video game can wait—how about if we play Scrabble now?"

My brother—such a brownnoser.

"Are you sure?" Mom asked. She looked so happy.

"Positive," I said. "We can't have a really late night, anyway. We want to be at the lifts first thing tomorrow morning. You know—to avoid the lines. We'll probably leave at five a.m., right, Frank?"

"Yup." Frank nodded. "Five o'clock in the morning sounds perfect."

"Wow, that is early," said Mom. "Joe, promise me you'll be more careful tomorrow?"

My brother turned to me and put his hand on my shoulder. "Mom's right, Joe. Even *I'm* starting to worry about you. You need to take it easy."

I smiled through gritted teeth and answered, "Promise."

As soon as Mom was out of earshot, I whispered, "I'll get you for that later."

Frank asked, "Is that supposed to be a threat?"

"Nope," I replied. "Just a promise."

4

The Lay of the Land

Even though the flight from Tahoe to Phoenix was less than two hours, it felt as if we'd traveled to a different universe. It wasn't just the climate—we were prepared to go from the frigid, cold mountains to a scorching-hot desert. But the thing is, there was nothing desertlike about the Billington Resort. There were lush green lawns and flowers everywhere.

"For a place that gets only eight to ten inches of rain a year, Phoenix sure feels tropical," I said.

"Yeah, this place is weird," Joe agreed.

The resort was so huge and sprawling, it took us almost twenty minutes just to get the lay of the land. There were twenty-three separate buildings, spread out over forty-five acres. Besides guest rooms, the hotel contained four ballrooms, five restaurants, and a beauty salon and spa. Outside, the grounds were filled with seven swimming pools, two golf courses, eight tennis courts, croquet courts, and even a cobblestone street lined with shops. With an ice cream parlor and a general store, it was set up to look like a small-town Main Street.

And the people? They were weird, too. The place was crawling with women dripping with fancy jewelry. Most of the guys were wearing pastel shorts and shirts. Basically, we were in a private, self-contained village for rich people.

The size of the place was astounding. It was so large, there could be five raging parties happening all at once, and they'd never overlap. It was hard to believe that a couple of guys could complain about sharing the place—even two ego-driven multimillionaires like Beller and Peterson.

"Know what I'm thinking?" asked Joe.

"No idea," I replied.

"Sure, it's hot out here, but what's with all the sun visors? Why not just get a hat that can protect your whole head, rather than leaving a gaping hole in the middle?"

I glared at my brother, but that didn't cut his rant any shorter.

"Especially bald guys in sun visors," he went on.

"What are they thinking? Do these guys know how stupid those things actually look?"

"I'm guessing no. Otherwise, they probably wouldn't be wearing them."

"Right," said Joe.

As we strolled past an Olympic-size swimming pool, Joe suddenly stopped short and grabbed my arm.

"Is that Cassandra Marquis?" he asked, pointing to some woman in a yellow bikini. She was lounging at the other end of the pool.

"Who?" I wondered.

"That actress on that new sitcom? I forget what it's called. You know what I'm talking about, though. She used to be in those potato chip commercials, too."

"I have no idea," I answered.

"Wow, you're really out of it." Joe slipped on his shades and walked toward the actress.

"Wait. Where are you going?" I asked, grabbing his arm.

"I want to talk to her," Joe replied.

I shook my head. "Come on, we can't. We're on a mission. And we're supposed to keep a low profile, remember?"

"Hey, this is all about the mission," said Joe. "She probably knows Beller. I'm hoping she'll give us some leads."

He shook himself free from my grasp and walked over to her. Or I should say, he *tried* to walk over to her. This beefy guy in a black T-shirt and a blond crew cut stopped him when he was still ten feet away.

"Do you know Ms. Marquis?" he asked, crossing his arms and glaring down at my brother.

"Uh, not personally," said Joe, backing up a few steps. "But I'm a huge fan."

"Ms. Marquis didn't come here to talk to fans," he said. "She came here so she could relax, in private."

"Okay," said Joe, holding up his hands in mock surrender. "I can take a hint. Sorry, dude." He headed back to me with his head down and his shoulders slumped.

I managed to refrain from saying "Told you so," and I didn't even laugh. Of course, I didn't have to. Someone else was cracking up. The voice was definitely female, and it was coming from right behind me.

I turned around to find this really pretty girl sitting by the pool. She had short blond hair and blue eyes. She was dressed in blue shorts and a pink tank top with matching flip-flops, and she was knitting a blue and red striped scarf.

When she noticed us watching her, she stopped

laughing. "Oh, I'm sorry. Don't take offense. It's just that I've been sitting here for less than an hour and you're the fourth guy I've seen try to approach Cassandra."

I finally had something to smile about. "Nice work, Joe."

The girl said, "If Cassandra Marquis pays her security guard by each nuisance he gets rid of, she's going to owe him a lot of cash at the end of the day."

"You may think I'm just another nuisance," said Joe. "But that's not the case at all. I figured that would happen. I just wanted to keep the security guard on his toes."

This time we all laughed.

"Joe Hardy," said my brother, offering her his hand. "And this is my brother, Frank."

"Nice to meet you. I'm Ashley McGill," she said, setting down her knitting needles and shaking both of our hands. "So are you guys with the wedding? Or are you here for the car show?"

"Neither," said Joe, as he sat down at the foot of Ashley's lounge chair. "We're just here with our parents for the weekend. What about you?"

"My parents dragged me here, too, but for the wedding," Ashley explained. "Ella Sinclair is my dad's cousin."

"Cool," I said.

"One would think," said Ashley. "But it's actually pretty boring here."

Joe shaded his eyes from the sun and squinted up at me. "Take a seat, Frank."

I sat down in the lounge next to them.

Joe picked up Ashley's scarf. "It's a little warm for this, don't you think?"

"Yes, here," she said. "But I go to school in Wisconsin."

"Wisconsin?" Joe exclaimed. "That is such a funny coincidence. I am a huge fan of cheese. . . ."

". . . and of being cheesy," I added.

I wasn't giving Joe a hard time for no reason. While he was using this opportunity to flirt, I realized we could actually get some potentially valuable information from Ashley. She was Ella Sinclair's cousin, after all.

"So, do you know Jake Beller?" I asked. Time to dial direct.

"Not really," Ashley said. "But I do know enough about him to know that I can't stand him."

"How come?" I wondered.

"He's a mega-huge developer," said Ashley. "And he's turned miles of beautiful Arizona desert into tract houses and shopping malls and parking lots."

"I guess everyone needs a place to live," said Joe.

"Not everyone needs a huge mansion with grass

and trees and flowers in the desert," said Ashley. "This country's focus on the new and overdone is kind of sickening, when you think about it. I mean, just look at his resort. Do you know how much water it takes to sustain all this grass and these flowers in their unnatural climate? Beller has only owned the Billington for six months, but he's already wasting twice as many natural resources as the old owners. Plus, he just bought up all the land surrounding the resort. He wants to build more houses and golf courses, like there aren't enough already. You know, this nonprofit group was trying to raise the funds to buy the land so they could turn it into a national park. But right before they signed the deal, Beller swept in and outbid them."

Ashley raised an interesting point. I wondered who owned all that land before Beller. Perhaps they were upset that he was developing it and adding to the suburban sprawl. "Which group was going to buy the land?" I asked.

"Don't know," said Ashley, with a shrug. "Hey, sorry to go off on such a tangent. Do you guys want to play lawn chess?"

"It depends," said Joe. "What's lawn chess?"

"It's like regular chess, except the pieces are all five feet tall," Ashley explained.

"Wouldn't desert chess be more appropriate?" I wondered out loud.

Ashley smiled at me. "Good point. But try and find desert in this desert. You'll have to travel pretty far. I suggest we make do with the resources we have."

"Actually, we should go," I said, as I stood up.

"We'll take a rain check, though," Joe added. He gave Ashley his cell phone number and told her to give him a call later.

"Will do," she said. "Where are you off to now? More celebrity stalking?"

"Not if I can help it," I said. "We're gonna go check out the car show."

"I thought you guys weren't here for that," Ashley said.

"We're not," Joe replied. "But, uh, we don't really golf and the tennis courts are all full, so we thought we'd check it out."

"Be careful," said Ashley. "I tried going yesterday, but they're really strict about who gets in. You need a pass and everything."

"So you never made it inside?" asked Joe.

"I didn't say that," Ashley replied, as she went back to her knitting. "It's not hard to sneak in. There's no one guarding the exit."

"Thanks for the tip," I told her.

"Anytime," Ashley said, as she waved good-bye. "See you two later."

"Definitely," Joe replied.

I stifled an eye roll until we'd turned around and walked away.

"You know, we should have told Ashley we were here for the car show," I said to Joe, once we were out of earshot. "We do have passes."

"You're right," said Joe. "We'll figure something out next time we see her. So what's our cover from now on?"

"We're high school students," I said.

"We're always high school students," said Joe. "In real life and when we're working for ATAC. Isn't that getting a little old?"

I thought my brother was joking, but I wasn't positive. Sometimes it's hard to tell with him. "Maybe. But now we're *local* high school students. There's a suburb nearby called Scottsdale. Langston is their biggest high school, and that's where we're from. We shouldn't pretend we're staying at the resort, because it's too easy to prove we're not. I'll bet Beller gave his security team access to the guest list."

"Okay, dude. Whatever you say," said Joe.

We walked past another fountain and then an

orchid garden. Finally, we got to the parking lot at the other end of the resort. We flashed our passes at security and strolled on in. The lot was filled with some of the coolest-looking cars I'd ever seen.

"Oh man, this is awesome," said Joe, running over to a bright blue Jaguar Roadster, circa 1966.

Personally, I was more impressed with the 1962 green Aston Martin GT. It was sandwiched between a silver Cadillac Eldorado from 1953 and a cherry red Ferrari 250 Europa from 1954.

Everything looked shiny and brand-new. I'd seen the occasional restored vintage sports car, but never so many all in one place. It was pretty awesome. The only thing that would have made it cooler was if they'd had vintage motorcycles on display as well.

Joe and I had the hottest tricked-out bikes at home. Anytime I was away from mine for more than a couple of days, I got itchy to ride.

After marveling at all the great-looking cars, I realized we had to get serious. It was already 10:30 a.m. That meant we had just three and a half hours to find the bomb before the resort would have to be evacuated. I pried Joe away from the bright yellow Cord 810 Supercharged Phaeton, circa 1937, so we could look for José Malrova, the chief of police in Phoenix.

We knew what he looked like from the research

we'd done online the night before. Chief Malrova was over six feet tall and he had wide shoulders, thick dark hair, and a heavy mustache. He also wore a tan Stetson cowboy hat, rather than a regular police officer's cap.

It didn't take us long to find him. It was just strange that he was standing on the other side of the street. We walked over to meet him and to find out what was up.

"I'm Frank Hardy," I said, shaking his hand. "And this is my brother, Joe. Mind if we ask you a few questions?"

Chief Malrova smiled. "You're Fenton's boys, right?"

"You know our dad?" asked Joe.

The police chief nodded. "I sure do. And I just spoke to him this morning. He told me you'd be coming out here, doing a little investigating. It didn't take me long to guess you were looking into the bomb threat. My officers have been working on this case all week, but we haven't made much progress. I've heard about you boys—you've got impressive reputations for amateurs. Plus, I'm glad to have someone on our team who can actually set foot on the Billington premises."

"We were wondering what you're doing out here," said Joe.

The police chief frowned and waved one hand toward the resort. "These rich guys. They think they're above the law. If only they'd let us handle things, I'm sure we'd have found the bomb by now."

"What do you mean?" I wondered.

"The Billington Resort is private property," Chief Malrova explained. "And Jake Beller has decided to prevent police from wandering the premises."

"Why wouldn't Beller want his resort protected?" I asked. "That's pretty strange, don't you think?"

"Maybe, maybe not," said the chief. "Beller has his own security force and I hear they're former CIA—some very tough men and women. And this place is insured for millions. It blows up, and Beller won't lose much. In fact, he may even profit from it."

"I can't imagine he'd want a bomb going off at his own wedding," said Joe. "And isn't this place plenty profitable on its own? We were in one of the gift shops a little while ago, and I saw this guy buying a T-shirt for eighty-five bucks."

Chief Malrova frowned and adjusted his cowboy hat. "Yes, Beller does make plenty of money on this property. I'm probably jumping to conclusions," he said. "Still, I have to wonder why he's being so difficult. A simple sweep of the grounds with our bomb-sniffing dogs would fix this situation."

"He said no to that?" I asked.

The police chief nodded. "Beller is deathly allergic to all things furry. Or so he says . . ."

"Which one is Henry Peterson?" I asked, shading my eyes with one hand and squinting toward the parking lot.

"The owner of the M&P Car Auction?" asked the chief. "He's right over there." The police chief pointed to a tall, heavy man with dark hair. He was wearing an old-fashioned gray car mechanic's jumpsuit and a red satin Indy 500 jacket. "Henry is a little more reasonable. Not much, though. He has his own security people too."

Near Henry were three men, all of whom were wearing dark suits. One held a walkie-talkie. Another had a lump in the pocket of his jacket that was so large it was obvious, even from where we were standing across the street, that he was carrying a gun.

"I wouldn't be surprised if Henry has undercover agents tooling around as well," said Chief Malrova. "Even if it weren't for the bomb threat, the M&P Car Auction always attracts thieves."

"What a mess," said Joe.

"True," I agreed. "But at least we'll have a lot of help if we need to evacuate."

"Don't count on it," said Chief Malrova. "Ready for the really bad news? Beller and Peterson don't think the bomb threat is real. Both of them think the other made it up to ruin their event. We'll try and get everyone out at two o'clock, but I'm afraid that many may not be willing to leave. Especially if the owner of the resort is telling them there's nothing to worry about. We can't force anyone out either. It's a free country."

"You're sure the bomb is real?" I asked.

"We're ninety-nine percent sure," said the police chief. "There were traces of ammonium nitrate found nearby. The FBI also intercepted communication from a terrorist group. We just don't know who they are, or where the bomb is—because unfortunately, the FBI bug malfunctioned right after they found out when the bomb is set to go off. We trust our information, but Beller and Peterson don't."

Joe and I definitely had our work cut out for us. "Thanks for filling us in, Chief Malrova," I said. "We'd better get to work."

"Good luck, boys," said the police chief. "You'll need it."

As we headed back across the street, Joe said,

"Let's split up. Is it okay with you if I talk with Henry Peterson?"

"Sure," I said. "I'll question his security team and anyone else I can find."

I checked my watch. It was already 10:50. "Let's try and do this quickly," I said. "We only have three hours and ten minutes to go."

5

Undercover

I couldn't wait to meet Henry Peterson. Problem was, I'd have to get by his security guards first. I'd learned my lesson from my non-encounter with Cassandra Marquis. If I wanted to gain access, I'd need a good cover story.

Or at least *a* cover story.

"Uh, excuse me," I said, walking past Henry's security guards like I didn't know who they were. "Mr. Peterson, I go to Langston High School in Scottsdale, and I'm writing an article for the school paper about your car auction. Would you mind if I asked you a few questions?"

Henry frowned. "I'm really busy here. It's not that I don't want to, but, uh, I don't think—"

I jumped in before he could actually say no. "Great, thanks," I said, pulling out my notebook. "It'll only take five minutes. I've read a lot about your career. It's so cool that you own the largest antique car auction house in the whole country."

"Actually," said Henry, "it's the largest in the world."

"Wow!" I bugged my eyes out, trying to look as impressed as possible. "That's so amazing. How did you get started?"

Now, I know that posing as a geeky high school reporter wasn't the most original cover, but since I didn't have time to think of anything great, I decided to fall back on a handy piece of conventional wisdom: People love talking about themselves. And this Henry guy was no exception.

"I've been interested in cars ever since I was a kid," he said.

Maybe I was imagining this, but I could have sworn that he puffed his chest out with pride.

"That's so fascinating," I said, just to encourage him.

"When I was four years old, I used to sit by the front window of my house, and I could guess the make of any car that drove down my street just by the sound of its engine," Henry continued. "And when I was six, I tried to drive my mother's old Buick. I managed to get the key in the ignition and put the car in drive. Problem was, my feet wouldn't reach the pedals. The car rolled down the driveway and across the street. It crashed right into our neighbor's mailbox, knocking the whole thing over, and I was lucky it stopped there."

That actually was kind of interesting. "So are you saying that you always wanted to own an antique car auction house?" I asked.

"Not exactly," Henry replied. "This all came about due to a series of happy accidents. See, I used to be a mechanic in Dallas. I specialized in old cars. I bought a Jaguar Roadster from the 1950s, fixed it up all by myself, and then sold it to the CEO of some oil company. Eventually I bought a used car dealership, and that did well, so I bought another. Soon I had a whole chain. All the while, I was collecting my own antique cars, but only one at a time.

"I had the idea for the auction about fifteen years ago. The first year it was in the parking lot of my used car dealership and I was unloading cars from my personal collection. A friend of mine asked me to include a few of his cars, so I did. The auction lasted only a couple of hours, and everything sold. My friend was so grateful, he gave me a cut of his profits. And that's when I had the idea for the auction. The next year I got more collectors involved and charged them all ten percent of their profits for my trouble. It was a win-win situation, because if their cars didn't sell, I took nothing. The auction got bigger and bigger every year. Now we're at this swanky hotel all week, and buyers come from all over the world. We have six auctions a year in six different cities."

"Wow, that's impressive," I said, looking up from my notes. I wasn't even acting anymore. Henry's business was cool. Come to think of it, he was too. "What's the most valuable car you have here?" I asked.

Henry scratched his stomach with one hand, then pointed to the southeast corner of the parking lot. "That's got to be the 1934 Duesenberg Model J Convertible Coupe. Fred and Augie Duesenberg were brothers from Indiana who built custom cars in the early 1900s. Since they're all hand built, they're very rare. This one's got an inline eight-cylinder engine, dual overhead camshafts, four valves per cylinder, a three-speed manual transmission, a front beam axle with a live rear axle and four-wheel, vacuum-assisted hydraulic brakes. It's a beautiful machine. It's a piece of art, really, except it's much better than artwork. What do you do with art but look at it? This art is beautiful *and* functional."

"It's cool looking. What do you think it'll go for?" I asked.

Henry frowned at the car. "Two million, minimum. Maybe a lot more. It's hard to tell, since I've actually never had one at the auction before."

"Two million dollars?" I repeated. "For one car?"

Henry nodded. "People spend more than that on Picassos. Why not cars?"

"Good point," I said.

"Want to come have a look under the hood?" he asked.

"I wish I had time," I said. I was working against a deadline and had to cut to the chase. "Hey," I said, "I heard that Jake Beller is getting married here this weekend. He's got enough cash to buy a car like that. Maybe he'll get it for his new bride."

Suddenly Henry's face went sour, like he'd just swallowed a mouthful of rotten milk. His eyes hardened and turned icy gray. "Actually, I was thinking about getting it for myself. Don't talk to me about Jake Beller. The way he's been treating me, he's lucky to still have my business. But he's not going to be so lucky for long."

It felt like the temperature had suddenly dropped twenty degrees.

"What do you mean by that?" I asked. "Are you not coming back here next year?"

"Oh, I'll be back," said Henry. "I'm not gonna let some New York City billionaire push me around. That's not how we do things in Texas."

My pen froze. I looked up at Henry and asked him very carefully, "How exactly do they do things in Texas, Mr. Peterson?"

Just then Henry looked at me kind of funny. "What high school did you say you went to?"

"Langston," I said, meeting his eyes with a steady gaze. "It's in Scottsdale."

Henry peered over his shoulder and glanced at Chief Malrova, who was still standing across the street. Then he nodded to one of his guards, who was talking with Frank.

"Best of luck with your story, kid," Henry said. "I'd really best be going now."

"Thank you for your time, sir. I'll send you a copy of the article when it comes out." I shook his hand and walked away quickly, figuring it was better not to press my luck.

I didn't know if Henry Peterson was guilty, but I was sure of one thing. After that interview, he was definitely suspicious of *me*.

6

Suspicion Grows

I was just finishing my interview with Maynard Smith, Henry's security guard, when I noticed that Joe and Henry Peterson were watching me. I hurried to wrap things up and got away from Smith as fast as I could.

I pretended to admire an old Corvette while watching my brother out of the corner of my eye. Moments later he shook Henry's hand and headed in the opposite direction from me.

When we were sure no one was watching us, but still within sight of each other, Joe signed the following message from across the parking lot: *I think Henry is on to me. I'm going to figure out a way to get close to Beller. You should stick around the auction, or it'll look too suspicious. Let's meet at the orchid garden in fifteen minutes.*

Sounds good, I signed back, silently thanking Mom for putting us through that sign language course.

As I continued to marvel, honestly, at the Corvette, I rethought the case. When Joe and I were on the plane to Phoenix, we'd discussed the possibility that the bomb threat was an inside job.

That still might be the case, but if it was, I was certain that it wasn't coming from Henry's security team. Maynard Smith hadn't given me any useful information. He and the other two guards were very chummy with Henry. They'd all been on Henry's payroll for five years, and apparently Henry treated them very well. They traveled with him to all six of his auctions every year. In their down time, they worked as mechanics at one of Henry's car dealerships in Dallas. Henry was even helping Maynard restore a Porsche from the 1970s that Maynard found in a junkyard.

According to Maynard, Henry had wanted to cooperate with the Phoenix police when news of the bomb threat first came out. It was Beller who refused to let the cops on the grounds, and since Beller owned the Billington, it was his decision.

At least that allowed me to cross three suspects off our list. I wandered through the auction for a few minutes but soon grew frustrated. I wasn't getting anywhere. The crowd seemed completely and legitimately into cars. As far as I could tell, no one had a sinister motive.

When I got to the foreign car section, I noticed a group of people about my age working on the cars. All of them were wearing the same uniform: khaki pants and a blue-collared shirt. The pocket of each shirt was embroidered with a small insignia: M&P, the initials of the car auction. I figured they were Henry's employees and that maybe they'd give me some leads.

As soon as I got close enough, this girl with dark hair and brown eyes introduced herself.

"Hi, there. I'm Maria Sanchez," she said.

"Nice to meet you. I'm Frank Hardy." I pointed toward the yellow Aston Martin that she was shining. "Nice car."

"This is one of the rarest," she said. "There are only twenty-eight of these exact cars left in the entire country."

"And I notice there are two at the auction. Wow, lucky for Henry Peterson," I replied.

"Actually, the other is not nearly as rare," said Maria. "But yes, he's a lucky guy."

"What do you think this one will go for?" I wondered. I knew from my research that even though the cars were all owned privately, Henry took a ten percent cut of the profits, as payment for auctioning them off.

"Well, I'm not supposed to say, but I would be shocked if it went for anything under a million," Maria said.

"A million dollars? On one car?" I asked.

Maria nodded. "People get crazy at these things."

I quickly did the math. A million-dollar sale meant a $100,000 profit for Henry. Not all of the cars would go for that much, but still, ten percent of the sale of 145 fancy old cars had to add up to a lot of cash.

Chief Malrova had raised a good point about Beller's insurance policy on the Billington Resort. Forgetting the danger and just focusing on the money, if the resort was destroyed, Beller wouldn't lose much. But if a bomb destroyed all of the cars at the M&P auction, Henry would get nothing. It's not like you can insure cars that don't belong to you. Plus, if people heard that Henry's Phoenix auction had attracted a terrorist, they might be reluctant to put their cars in his five others. It could ruin his whole business. And while Beller had at least ten companies and *The Candidate,* his own reality television show, Henry Peterson had only his auction.

Would Peterson really risk all that just to get back at Jake Beller? It was hard to imagine. . . .

"So, have you been to many other auctions?" I asked.

"Oh sure," said Maria. "My dad has a garage nearby. We've been working on cars together since I was six years old. I've been coming to the M&P auction for years."

"And how long have you been working for Henry?"

"This is my third year," Maria replied.

"Do you like it? Are these auctions decent places to work?" I asked. "What's Henry like?"

Maria tilted her head to one side and stared up at me. Her pretty brown eyes sparkled in the sun. "You sure have a lot of questions," she said.

Whoops. "Oh, sorry. It's just that I'm really into vintage cars and would love to work for M&P. Any advice on how I can do that?"

"Well, you should definitely drop your résumé off with Henry," said Maria. "And I'll put in a good word." She finished shining the hood of the car and put her rag in her back pocket. "Why don't you come and meet some of the other car handlers?" she asked.

Perfect, I thought, following Maria to the rest of the group. She introduced me to three guys: Justin Jones, Douglas Selby, and Tanner McCarthy. They were all high school students from different schools in Phoenix. Luckily for me, none of them went to Langston in Scottsdale.

"So, what's a typical day of work here at the auction?" I asked.

"It depends," said Justin. "Most of our work happens before the auction. We wash and clean the inventory, which takes forever. The actual viewing hours, when this is all open to the public, can be very tricky. We're responsible for keeping the cars clean—and you'd be surprised by how many people leave fingerprints everywhere."

"The actual auction is the most fun," said Douglas. "We're the ones who get to drive the cars up on stage."

It sounded like they had lots of access to the cars and to the resort in general. But did any of them have a motive to blow it all up? It didn't seem that way.

As we were talking, though, I noticed something strange. Tanner's shirt was a little different from the others. I had to look for a while before I finally figured out why. Then it hit me. Rather than an M&P,

Tanner's shirt was embroidered with an M&B.

Unfortunately, he caught me staring.

"My regulation shirt disappeared," he said. "I couldn't tell Henry because he'd get really mad, so I managed to pick this one up at a secondhand shop."

"That's a good fake," I replied.

"That's what I thought, until I saw you staring," said Tanner, crossing his arms over his chest to hide the fake logo. "I've been wearing it all week, and you're the first person to notice."

Something about the way he said it left me wondering. And experience has taught me that it's often those who are the most suspicious themselves who end up being guilty.

"How long have you been working for Henry, Tanner?" I asked.

"Six months," he said. "Through the organizational stages, and now, at the auction. I've been with Henry ever since my family moved to Phoenix from Baltimore."

Before I could ask him anything else, he said, "It's been nice talking with you, Frank, but we need to get back to work. Don't you think, Maria?"

She nodded. "Tanner is right. We don't want to get caught goofing off. Henry is a good boss for the

SUSPECT PROFILE

Name: Henry Peterson

Hometown: Dallas, Texas

Physical description: 42 years old, 6'2", large stomach, pale skin, dark hair. People say he always wears an Indy 500 jacket over a mechanic's jumpsuit.

Occupation: Owner of M&P Car Auction

Background: Started out as a mechanic, then bought a car dealership, and then a chain of car dealerships, until he started the auction fifteen years ago.

Suspicious behavior: Threatened Jake Beller and challenged him to a fistfight. (Beller refused.)

Suspected of: Planting a bomb at the Billington Resort.

Possible motives: This guy is ego-driven. He doesn't care how much money Jake Beller has. He resents that Jake tried to bribe him. He's had his car auction on the same weekend at the same resort for fifteen years, and he's not gonna budge.

most part, but he has a really bad temper. Once he starts yelling, it just builds and builds. . . . He's totally explosive."

"Really?" I asked, raising my eyebrows. *Explosive* sure was an interesting choice of words.

Maria nodded and winked at me. "Yup. But I'm here all weekend, so just drop by whenever with your résumé."

I sneaked a look at Tanner, who rolled his eyes. Then I smiled at Maria, pretending like I hadn't noticed. "Sounds good," I said. "Thanks for your time."

I waved good-bye and then headed to the orchid garden.

I still had a few minutes before Joe was supposed to show, so I leaned up against a wall and pulled my notebook from my back pocket. So Henry was *explosive*? I wondered if Maria was hinting at something. She *had* winked.

At the moment Tanner McCarthy was the only one I could legitimately add to my list of suspects. His shirt was a big red flag, and something about his excuse seemed a little fishy. I did have to wonder, would he actually blow the entire resort to smithereens? And what kind of motive could a seventeen-year-old high school senior possibly have?

I was just writing down the question, when a heavy shadow loomed over me.

It was Tanner. He'd followed me out.

"Hey, Hardy," he said gruffly.

I quickly flipped my notebook shut. "Hi, Tanner. While you're here, maybe you can help me out. I just thought of one more question. Do M&P employees travel from show to show? Or do you guys just handle the Phoenix auction? See, I really want to work for M&P, but I have a pet dog and I can't leave her overnight because she has this nervous condition. Whenever we're apart for more than a day, she starts chewing on her own tail."

For some reason Tanner was looking really mad. "Aw, cut it out, man. I know you're not really trying to get a job here."

"You do?" I asked.

He laughed, but it wasn't a "ha-ha, you're so funny" kind of laugh. It was more like a "ha-ha, I'm gonna kick your butt" laugh. "It's so obvious," he said.

"I don't know what you're talking about," I said.

Tanner took a step closer and replied in a tone that told me he meant business. "We both know exactly what I'm talking about. I'm not going to say anything, but just know that I'm on to you. You

SUSPECT PROFILE

Name: Tanner McCarthy

Hometown: Phoenix, Arizona

Physical description: 17 years old, 5'11", blond hair, brown eyes, wiry build.

Occupation: High school student and part-time car handler at the M&P Car Auction

Background: Moved to Phoenix from Baltimore, Maryland. Has been working at the auction for six months.

Suspicious behavior: His shirt is obviously a fake. It has an M&B logo on it, rather than M&P. He's also really paranoid—he noticed Frank looking at his fake uniform and came up with an excuse right away. Later on, he threatened Frank.

Suspected of: Planting a bomb that will blow up the Billington Resort.

Possible motives: No idea, unless maybe Henry Peterson or Jake Beller put him up to it.

think you can get in the way of this, but you can't. And now that I know what you're doing, you'd better watch your back."

I kept my face as deadpan as possible. He obviously wasn't buying my cover, but I still wasn't going to blow it.

When it was clear that I wasn't going to say anything else, he walked away. I glanced down at my notebook and underlined his name. Okay. I still wasn't sure of Tanner's motive, but obviously the guy was guilty of something.

7

Operation Bobo

My meeting with Henry hadn't given me much to work with. As far as I could tell, he was a nice guy. A little puffed up and arrogant, maybe, but certainly not a terrorist. Furthermore, he seemed totally decent. It was hard to imagine that anyone would be angry enough with him to blow his entire business to smithereens.

I really hoped we'd have better luck with Ella and Jake. Being soon-to-wed celebrities, though, it's not like they were going to be standing around a parking lot, or anywhere near as approachable as Henry. I'd come up with a great way to get close to them, but first I needed to get Frank up to speed. I pulled out my notebook and a pen so I could write some things down on my way to our meeting spot.

When I made it to the orchid garden, Frank was already there.

"So what's the story with Henry?" he asked, as soon as he saw me.

"Yes, the dude has a serious grudge against Jake Beller," I said. "But I don't think he'd resort to violence. He seems fairly harmless."

Remembering something else, I went back to my notebook.

"Are you adding new suspects to the list?" Frank asked. "Because I have one I need to tell you about."

"Nope, this isn't a suspect list," I said.

"So what is it?"

I handed him the notebook and explained, "You need to do some studying before our next meeting."

Frank read my list out loud. "*Legally Insane, One Bullet Junction, Dangerous Games, Two to Tango*, an infomercial for the revolutionary machine that whitens teeth with the electric toothbrushlike device, now available for purchase in just three monthly installments of $19.98."

Frank looked at me like I was crazy. (It was something I was used to by now.) "What is this?" he asked.

"It's a list of movies that Ella has been in. Oh,

and the infomercial. She filmed it when she was starting out and desperate a few years ago, but they reissued it recently to capitalize on her success. Actually, that's something you shouldn't bring up. It's probably upsetting. She starred in *Two to Tango*. I'm sure she'd love to talk about that."

"What are you talking about?" Frank asked.

"You should really study up, so you don't embarrass yourself."

Frank threw the notebook back at me and said, "Joe, this is nuts. It's eleven fifteen. We're running out of time. You have got to take this more seriously."

"This is *very* serious," I insisted. "Actors have crazy egos. Trust me. If you don't know her work, she's gonna be insulted. This is the easiest way in."

My brother groaned and said, "Sometimes I wonder how it's possible that we share DNA."

"You're not the only one who wonders about that," I replied. "Come on, let's go to the spa. Beller and Ella have massages booked in fifteen minutes. I'm hoping we can talk to them before."

"Okay, but remember, Beller's security are all ex-CIA. I'll bet they're really intense. They're not going to just let us into the spa," Frank said.

Oops. Looks like I forgot to fill my brother in on some of the details. "Um, don't worry about that.

We'll get in, no problem. I booked us appointments for around the same time." I kept my answer vague, hoping that Frank didn't ask too many more questions.

Frank nodded and said, "Okay, that sounds good, but don't massages take a full hour? There's no way we have time for that."

"I know," I said. "My original plan was to book the massages and then slip out after we spoke to Beller."

"What do you mean, 'your original plan'?" asked Frank.

My brother doesn't miss a thing—too bad for me. We were almost at the spa and he was going to find out soon anyway, so I decided to come clean. "Uh, all the masseurs were booked, so I had to get us other appointments. You're getting a sports pedicure at twelve fifteen."

Frank stopped in his tracks. "You did *not* book me for a pedicure, Joe. Tell me you're kidding. I know this is a big case, but I am not going around this place with painted nails!"

"I just told you, it's a *sports* pedicure. It's for guys. No painted nails."

"I can't believe I left you in charge of getting us a meeting with Beller," Frank grumbled as he threw his arms up in the air.

"Hey, you should be thanking me. This is gonna work. Trust me. Plus, I'm the one who's stuck with something called an aromatherapy facial."

"But I still have to go to the spa and say, 'Hi, I'm here for a pedicure.'"

"*Sports* pedicure," I reminded him again. "And we're not sticking around for the appointments anyway, so relax."

"Whatever. That is not cool," said Frank.

When we got to the spa and added our names to the sign-in sheet, I noticed that Beller and Ella's names were already there.

"Told you so," I whispered to Frank.

"Whatever," he replied.

"Let's see," said the woman behind the counter. "Frank and Joe—that's one aromatherapy facial and one pedicure, right?"

"That's supposed to be a *sports* pedicure," Frank said.

The woman smiled and glanced down at her appointment book. "Oh, excuse me. You're right." She reached down under the counter and pulled out two fluffy white robes. "Changing rooms are in back. After you put these on, you'll go to the waiting room. There's fresh orange juice, water, and tea in there. Please help yourselves. We'll call you when we're ready for you."

"Wait, no one ever said anything about a robe," said Frank. "I'm not wearing that thing."

"It's spa policy," said the woman. "If you don't wear it, you can't go in."

I elbowed my brother. "He's just kidding. Of course he'll wear it. We're both thrilled to be getting these things, so thank you." I took both robes and tucked them under my arm.

"Enjoy," said the woman.

I shot Frank a warning look and he pasted on a fake smile. "Thank you," he said. "We sure will."

As we headed into the dressing room, I said, "Just keep your clothes on underneath. That way we can make a quick getaway."

"I can't believe I let you talk me into this," he replied.

I understood where my brother was coming from. Yesterday we were shredding down Doomed River Run at breakneck speeds. And today we were at a spa? Our work at ATAC has taken us to some strange places—and the Billington Resort was by far one of the strangest.

We left our shoes and socks in a locker and slipped into the spa's flip-flops. Then we rolled our jeans up above our knees and put on the robes.

"We'd better not run into anyone we know," said Frank.

"We're two thousand miles away from home," I reminded my brother. "Who do you think we're going to see?"

"Stranger things have happened," Frank replied.

"You need to chill," I said, as we headed to the waiting room.

Bingo! Beller and Ella were already in there. It was funny. I'd seen them plenty of times on television, and I'd never missed any of Ella's movies. But seeing them in person, in white, fluffy robes? It wasn't what I was expecting. Beller looked much older than he did on TV. Ella was still beautiful, with shoulder-length black hair, blue eyes, and pale, Snow White skin. But she looked like a regular person, rather than a glamorous movie star. I don't know what I was expecting—a silvery glow surrounding her body, maybe? Who knows?

They were speaking in hushed voices. Frank and I sat on either side of them so we could listen in. I made sure to take the seat next to Ella because, well, just because . . .

"I just don't understand why you want to seat your publicist at the head table," said Beller.

"You wouldn't," Ella said with a huff. "But since two of your ex-wives are here, I don't really feel like you can argue with me about an issue as small as the seating."

"If it's such a small issue, then why are you so worked up about it?" asked Beller.

"You're impossible," Ella hissed back.

"Funny," Beller replied, as he picked up his paper. "I was just thinking the same thing about you."

When Ella went back to reading her book, I found my in.

"That's one of my favorites," I said. "What part are you on?"

"Oh," she said, pulling her robe tighter around her. "Are you a big fan of Ernest Hemingway?" she asked.

"The biggest," I said. "We just read *A Farewell to Arms* in English class. It was amazing. Actually, it reminds me of this movie I just saw. It was sort of a modern version of the same story, except the soldier was played by a woman and she's in the Middle East instead of Europe. Maybe you've seen it—*Two to Tango*."

Ella's face lit up like a Christmas tree. "You saw that?"

"Yeah, did you?" I asked. "If not, you really should. The performances in it were truly amazing."

"Actually," she said, as her smile got even wider, "I was in it."

"*No!*" I acted as surprised as possible. "Wait a second. Are you—"

"Ms. Sinclair," said the masseuse who'd just popped her head into the room. "We're ready for you now."

"Thanks," said Ella, standing up and waving good-bye. "See you later."

I was sad to see her go, but Ella wasn't a suspect in this—and I had to stay focused. According to ATAC intelligence, she didn't even care if she had to share the resort. This was all about a feud between Beller and Peterson.

And now we were alone with Beller. Well, practically alone. There was another woman in the waiting room, sitting by the door—but she was absorbed in the latest issue of *Cigar Aficionado* magazine.

I discretely signed to my brother, *I told you so*.

He shook his head and discretely signed back, *I don't think flirting with Beller's fiancée is going to make the guy so eager to talk to you.*

I replied, *I wasn't flirting. I was just being friendly.*

Just then Beller pulled a cell phone out of his robe pocket and dialed a number. "It's me," he said quietly. "Ready to launch Operation Bobo."

My eyebrows shot up. Operation Bobo? If that wasn't suspicious, I don't know what is. I wondered if Bobo was some kind of acronym. If so, what could it stand for? Billington Operation Bomb Ordered? Bomb on Billington Orchestrated?

We had to get more information. But for now, all we could do was listen.

Beller said, "Yes, now, and you'd better hurry." Then he hung up his phone, slipped it into his pocket, and went back to reading his paper.

The guy seemed awfully calm. If only I could make Beller mad. *That* would get him talking.

I called to Frank, "That Aston Martin was pretty amazing, huh? This is one of the best car auctions I've ever been to."

"Excuse me, boys," said Beller, peering over the top of his newspaper. "This isn't a car auction. This is a spa, at one of the finest luxury resorts in the nation."

"Which also happens to be hosting the biggest car show in the world," I pointed out. "Have you seen it?"

"I have not, and I have no intention of ever seeing it," said Beller. "And the fact that my resort is crawling with mechanics on my wedding day is infuriating."

His cheeks were starting to flush. My plan was working.

"You're missing out," said Frank. "This is a killer car auction."

What Beller said next totally surprised us. "That's an ironic choice of words."

"How so?" I asked.

"Never mind," Beller replied. He raised his paper back up so that it was covering his face, but before he did, I noticed he was smiling. "Enjoy it while you can, boys. Henry Peterson and his little auction aren't going to be around forever. I've made sure of that."

Frank and I locked eyes. It was clear we were thinking the same thing. Unbelievable—Beller had practically confessed to the crime.

Before I could even ask him anything else, he was called away for his massage. I tried following him out of the waiting room so I could get more details, but the only other person in the room stopped me.

It was the other lady in the waiting room, who'd been reading *Cigar Aficionado*. I can't believe we didn't think she might be Beller's undercover security guard before! Too late now. She was standing in front of the door, blocking our exit. "Where do you boys think you're going?" she asked.

"I have a question for Mr. Beller," Frank said.

"Mr. Beller isn't taking any questions now," the woman replied. "And don't even think about trying to get past me. I'm trained in four different types of

SUSPECT PROFILE

<u>Name:</u> Jake Beller

<u>Hometown:</u> New York City

<u>Physical description:</u> 65 years old, 5'10", but he tells the press he's over 6 feet tall. Thin with red hair and a bad toupee. He always wears expensive dark suits and shiny black shoes. Usually wears sunglasses, even inside.

<u>Occupation:</u> Real estate developer and reality television star

<u>Background:</u> Started buying and selling real estate in the seventies. Was once bankrupt. This will be his fourth wedding, but only his second time marrying a model/actress.

<u>Suspicious behavior:</u> Tried to get the M&P Car Auction to change the date. Offered a bribe and then threatened to sue. Finally gave up but told Henry Peterson, "If you go through with this, you'll be sorry."

<u>Suspected of:</u> Planting a bomb or faking a very convincing bomb threat.

<u>Possible motives:</u> Revenge. Ego. This guy is used to getting what he wants, when he wants it.

martial arts, and all of them are potentially lethal."

Yikes!

Just then the woman from the front desk came back into the room and said, "Frank and Joe Hardy? I'm sorry for the delay, but we're ready for you."

Phew! Saved by the spa lady. "Actually," I said, pulling Frank away, "we just got pedicures and facials yesterday. We're going to cancel our appointments."

Canceling was easy, but as it turned out, getting changed—or leaving—was not. Just as we were about to push open the door, the guard grabbed Frank by the lapels of his robe. "I know who you are," she said.

Sheesh. Everyone thought they knew who we were. It was like we were wearing signs on our backs: UNDERCOVER BROTHERS: ASK US WHO WE'RE WORKING FOR.

"We're just a couple of kids on vacation with our parents," Frank insisted. "I'm sorry I tried to talk to Beller. I've just never seen anyone famous in person before. I was excited. It won't happen again, though. I promise."

The guard loosened her grip on Frank's robe with a final warming. "You'd better make sure of that. I'm letting you go this time, because I want you to deliver a message to your boss."

"Our boss?" asked Frank.

"Yeah, your boss over at the M&P auction. You're obviously Henry's spies. Tell him it's no use. It's too late. No one messes with Jake Beller and gets away with it. We gave him fair warning, but he didn't listen. Now he's gonna learn his lesson the hard way."

"Okay, we'll let him know," I blurted out. "Just let us go."

Once she dropped Frank, we ran back to the locker rooms, ditched the robes and flip-flops, and put our shoes back on.

"What the heck is Operation Bobo?" I asked as soon as we were alone.

"I don't know," said Frank as he tied his shoelaces. "But I have a feeling something big is about to go down."

"We'd better warn Henry," I said.

"My thoughts exactly," Frank replied.

We hurried over to the car auction but had gone only a few steps when we heard a deafening explosion.

I felt the heat on my face before I even realized what was happening. As soon as it registered, I couldn't believe it. A heavy, black cloud of smoke rose up to the sky. Large, shooting flames were spewing from the parking lot.

Frank and I sprinted to the auction. All I could think about was one thing: The bomb had gone off early.

We were too late.

8

Fatal Mistakes

When we finally made it back to the parking lot, we were met with chaos. The fire, the screaming, the deafening sirens, and blackened faces—it was all too much to take in. We'd failed, big-time. And who knew how much damage had been done?

I wanted to help but wasn't sure where to start.

There were people everywhere. Some were frozen in shock, while others wandered around in a daze.

Fire trucks and ambulances were just pulling into the parking lot.

Chief Malrova and a bunch of his officers were already on the scene. I guess now that something had actually happened, Beller couldn't legally keep the police off his property.

"What was that?" I asked.

"Car bomb," Chief Malrova replied. "Much smaller than what we were expecting, but still, it was a doozy. It must have been in the Duesenberg, because all that's left of that car is the charred and twisted frame."

"Wow, that was the most valuable car at the auction," said Joe. "Henry is going to be ticked."

"No, he's not," said the chief.

"Sure he is," said Joe. "He loves that car. I should go find him, actually."

"Joe, wait." Chief Malrova put his hand on Joe's shoulder, stopping him in his tracks. "I have some very bad news. Henry Peterson was in the car at the time of the explosion. He's been killed."

"Wh—what?" Joe choked out the word as he staggered backward. "That's impossible. I was just talking to the guy."

"Has anyone else been killed?" I asked.

"Not that we know of yet," said the chief. "But it looks like there are plenty of injuries around here. More paramedics are on the way."

I scanned the crowd. A woman sat on the ground cradling her arm—it looked broken. The man next to her looked like he was suffering from a dislocated shoulder. A few feet away another guy with a cut above the eyebrow stood with a look of shock on his face. All four of the car handlers I'd met—Maria, Tanner, Douglas, and Justin—were huddled together and covered in soot. Otherwise, they seemed unscathed. Maynard Smith and Henry's other two security guards were also safe. That was a relief.

Just then I noticed that Joe was looking sort of queasy. I clapped a hand on his shoulder and asked, "You okay?"

"I just spoke to Henry," Joe said. "He pointed out the Duesenberg specifically. He was so proud of that car. It makes perfect sense that it would be a target, but I didn't even think to search for a bomb."

"Joe, this isn't your fault," I said.

He shook his head. "I should have paid closer attention. I should have asked him more about the car. He wanted to show me the engine, and I said no. If I was closer, if I'd looked under the hood, I'm sure I would have noticed there was something wrong. I could have stopped this."

"There's no way you could have known," said the police chief. "You tried your best."

"Chief Malrova is right," I said. "You can't blame yourself."

I wondered if the traces found by ATAC were of the same bomb-making material that was used to orchestrate this catastrophe. And was this the worst of it, or was there more to come?

I also wondered if Tanner had anything to do with all this. Maybe Beller had put him up to it. Tanner had been in Phoenix for only six months. Maybe his whole move was for this very purpose. Maybe he wasn't a high school student with a part-time job. If only I could establish some sort of link between Tanner and Beller . . .

I watched Tanner from afar. He had his arm around Maria, and her face was buried in his shoulder. I had to talk to the guy.

"I'll be right back," I said, heading toward the car handlers.

As soon as I got to Maria, she tore herself away from Tanner and gave me a big hug. "Frank, I'm so glad you're safe. Can you believe this?"

"No," I said. "It's too awful. Where were you guys during the explosion?"

"Well, five minutes before, we were all waxing the Duesenberg," said Douglas. "But then Tanner asked us to follow him to the stage so we could have a quick meeting."

"He saved us," said Maria. "We're so lucky."

Lucky? It sounded to me like they were purposely spared. But I wasn't going to say anything. Not until I had the evidence proving that Tanner planted the bomb.

"What was the meeting about?" I asked.

"Um, we never got that far," said Douglas. "We were interrupted by the explosion."

I had a lot of questions for Tanner, but the guy had suddenly disappeared. I'd taken my eyes off him for only a few seconds, too. I looked around, asking, "Where did Tanner go?"

The other car handlers seemed just as perplexed as me. "Don't know," said Douglas. "He was just here."

It was all too much of a coincidence. I had to find him. "Hey, I'm glad you guys are okay," I said, as I backed away. "I'll see you in a few."

I finally tracked Tanner down over by the stage. He was deep in conversation with Maynard Smith.

"Hey," I said. "Sorry about your boss."

"I still can't believe it," said Maynard. There were tears in his eyes. "I feel like I failed him. This was so unexpected. But really—who would want to hurt Henry?"

"That's an excellent question," I replied, staring pointedly at Tanner. "What do you think?"

"I don't know," said Tanner, eyeing me. "And I don't like what you're implying."

"Does Operation Bobo ring any bells?" I asked.

Tanner laughed in my face and asked, "Dude, what are you talking about?"

Maynard looked back and forth between me and Tanner and asked, "What's going on with you two?"

"Nothing," Tanner replied. "Right, Hardy?"

"Right," I said, rubbing my forehead. Were my instincts entirely off?

From the doubtful expression on his face, I could tell that Maynard didn't believe us. "Did you say 'Operation Bobo'?" he asked me. "What's that?"

"Nothing," I replied, staring down at the pavement.

Tanner said, "I'm going to find Maria. Don't even think about following me, Hardy." He stalked off.

"Hold up. I need to ask you something." I started after him, but Maynard stopped me.

"I don't think that's a good idea," Maynard said. "At least give him time to cool off."

"Cool off about what?" I asked. "He has no reason to be mad at me. It makes no sense. Don't you think there's something suspicious about all of his hostility?"

"Not really," said Maynard.

"All I did was ask a few questions earlier this morning about what it's like to work for the M&P auction. And he just automatically hates me? It makes no sense."

"Look, I don't know what's going on with Tanner, but maybe this isn't the best place for you to work. There are a lot of jobs in Phoenix," Maynard said. "Why make trouble at the auction? Especially now, in light of everything . . ."

"The M&P auction is the best," I said. "Why *wouldn't* I want to work here?"

Maynard stared at me. "Okay, wait. You really have *no* idea what this is about?"

I shook my head. "None whatsoever."

"You haven't noticed that Tanner's girlfriend has been flirting with you all morning?" he asked.

"Tanner's girlfriend?" I asked. Wait a second . . . Suddenly it was all clicking into place. "Tanner and Maria are a couple?"

"Yes," said Maynard. "Or at least they were until you showed up."

Wow, no wonder he was so mad at me. But it's not like I could explain that I had no interest in Maria or in working at the M&P auction without blowing my cover.

I still wasn't positive that Tanner was innocent— but obviously, I was going to have to be more subtle in my investigation of him. "Honestly, I didn't realize," I told Maynard. "Thanks for the heads-up."

"Anytime," Maynard replied.

I said good-bye and went looking for my brother.

When I found Joe, he and Chief Malrova were still talking about Henry's death and debating whether or not they should shut down the entire auction.

"It's definitely a safety hazard," said the chief.

"But Henry would probably have insisted that the show go on," Joe replied.

"You're probably right," said the chief. "And Maynard told me the same thing. I suppose that letting things move forward is the least we can do for Henry."

"Yeah," said Joe, his voice a gruff whisper. "I think it's a good idea."

My brother seemed really upset about Henry's death. Poor guy.

Just as I was about to start consoling my brother, my cell phone rang. My first instinct was to ignore it. Obviously, my brother's well-being was more important than whoever was calling. But at the same time, we *were* still on a case. Maybe ATAC headquarters was calling with new information. Or maybe they were kicking us off the case, since we were doing such a lousy job.

I took a few steps away from my brother and Chief Malrova before answering. "Hello?"

"Frank Hardy," said a muffled, slightly spooky voice. "Is that you?"

"Yes, who is this?" I asked.

"What did you think of the explosion? It was pretty cool, huh?"

I felt the hair on the back of my neck stand up. "Who is this?" I asked again.

The person at the other end of the line started laughing like a maniac. "I'm not telling. I just wanted to let you know that we're serious. The Duesenberg is only the beginning. This isn't over yet."

The phone went dead, leaving me with silence in my ear. Chills ran up and down my spine. I turned to my brother, but he was still talking to Chief Malrova.

"Joe," I said. "Hey, Joe?" I tugged at his sleeve.

"Yeah?" he asked, finally turning to me.

"That phone call I just took? It was the bomber. We're not done yet. . . ."

9

Surprise from Bayport

"Tell us the story, Frank," I said. "What's going on?"

When my brother finally recovered from the shock of the call, he told us about it. The news left me feeling angry, sad, and freaked out all at once.

I don't know why I was letting Henry's sudden death get to me so much. Maybe it was all those stories about his childhood. But I knew I had to shake myself out of this funk. There was no time for mourning. We had to make sure no more innocents were harmed. (I was assuming that Henry was innocent—but even if he wasn't, no one deserves to be killed, period.)

"Did you recognize the voice at all?" I asked.

"Impossible. It was way too muffled," Frank

explained, as he pressed some buttons on his phone. "And it looks like the number was blocked from my caller ID too."

"No surprise there," said Chief Malrova, tipping back his Stetson. "But don't worry. We've still got a chance. This guy knows who you are, and obviously, he wants attention. I bet he calls back."

"But from the same blocked number," Frank pointed out.

The chief of police nodded. "True, but our department has the technology to get around that problem. Follow me, boys."

Chief Malrova led us to his car and opened up the trunk. He pulled out two small, black rectangular boxes. Each one had a screen, like a matchbook-size television. "These are call tracers," the chief explained. "They have their own internal Global Positioning Systems. If you put one on your phone, it'll track down your caller's location."

Chief Malrova clipped the device onto Frank's phone and turned it on. A map of the resort appeared on the tiny screen. There was a green dot indicating where we were.

"Cool," I said.

"Yes, it is cool," the police chief said. "It's also highly functional."

He asked for Frank's number, walked a few steps away, and then dialed.

Almost as soon as the phone started to ring we saw a tiny, blinking red dot, showing where Chief Malrova was standing.

"What do you think?" asked the chief when he came back.

"Excellent," I said.

"This'll be helpful if the caller tries me again," Frank added, examining the tracer. He looked up at Chief Malrova and me. "And that's assuming the caller is close enough. What if we can't get to him or her in time? What if the caller moves?"

"That's the really innovative thing about these devices," said Chief Malrova. He walked about five yards in the other direction and turned left. "Take a look at the screen, boys," he called.

The red light actually traced his steps. When Malrova jogged toward us, the red dot flashed in time with his steps.

"The phone connection triggers an infrared tracing device. The marker will linger for fifteen minutes after the caller hangs up," Chief Malrova explained. "And whoever planted that bomb is no more than fifteen minutes away. That much I'm sure of."

"How do you know?" I asked.

"Experience," said Chief Malrova. "The terrorist worked too hard and cares too much. He knows this place is crawling with cops and private security. His phone call, and the fact that he knows who you guys are, proves that he's watching you. He's not going to disappear until he's sure his plan is played out."

"Okay," said Frank. "So what are we supposed to do until then?"

"Let's lie low for a while," I said. "Beller should be getting out pretty soon. All we need to do is stay close, come up with an excuse to talk to him, and figure out what this Operation Bobo thing is all about."

"Watch your back, boys," said Chief Malrova. "We're obviously dealing with a ruthless killer. I'd hate to see either of you get hurt."

"We'll be careful," I promised.

Frank said, "Will you keep an eye on Tanner McCarthy, also? He's one of Henry's car handlers. I have a hunch he's linked to Beller in some way."

"Sure thing," said Chief Malrova.

"Thanks," Frank replied.

We said good-bye to the chief and headed away from the parking lot mess.

We'd gone only a few steps when we heard someone call out, "What the heck are you two clowns doing here?"

The voice was all too familiar.

Frank groaned. "Do *not* tell me Brian Conrad is here."

I looked over my shoulder. "I could tell you he's not if you really want to hear it, but I'd be lying."

Just when I thought that things couldn't get any worse, they did. Brian Conrad was the biggest jerk in Bayport. Running into him in Phoenix, while we were on a top secret mission? It was a total nightmare.

Of course, he'd already spotted us, so we had to talk to him. We both turned around.

"Hey, Brian," Frank said.

"Did you guys see the explosion?" Brian asked. His eyes were shining and he had a sick smile pasted on his face. "It was so awesome. Stuff went flying and there was glass and smoke everywhere. The guy in the car must have been blown to bits. Man, that was cool."

"A guy died," I said, feeling my throat get tight. "There's nothing cool about that."

"Dude, why are you so serious all the time?"

asked Brian. "You need to chill. And what are you doing here, anyway?"

"We're on a family vacation," Frank said.

"I thought you guys were supposed to be skiing in Tahoe," said Brian.

"There was a change of plans," I said. "Our dad twisted his ankle and he can't ski on it, so we came here instead. We're supposed to meet our parents on the croquet courts in a little while."

"Whatever," said Brian. "Don't let me stop you."

"Hey, how did you know we are supposed to be in Tahoe?" I asked.

I was a little paranoid, but it wasn't without reason. Brian tends to show up at the most inconvenient times. He'd gotten in the way of too many missions. Sometimes I wondered if he was on to us.

Brian rolled his eyes. "For some dumb reason, Belinda likes to keep track of these things. Don't ask me why. I keep telling her not to waste her time, but my sister is stubborn."

"Is she here?" I asked.

"She and my mom are at the spa," said Brian.

Great. Not only did we have no idea who was behind the bomb, there was also a chance that Belinda Conrad saw us in white, fluffy robes. Did I mention how cute she was? The last thing I wanted was for a cute girl to see me looking like a fool. Not that she ever noticed me, anyway. Everyone knew Belinda had a major crush on Frank.

Well, everyone except for Frank, that is. He wouldn't admit it.

"Let's go," said Frank.

"Hold on a second," I replied. "What are you doing here, Brian?"

"I'm here for the car auction. What else? My dad is selling his old BMW 507. Come on, I'll show it to you."

Brian led us over to a bright red convertible. I hate to admit it, but it was an awesome ride. It was in mint condition, with shiny chrome fenders and a black-and-white leather interior. Even the radio looked authentic.

"It's from 1957. Only a hundred fifty-three were ever made," Brian told us as he leaned against the hood of the car. "Dad and I have been working on it together for a couple of years now, rebuilding the engine and stuff."

Suddenly someone started shouting. "Brian, what the heck are you doing? I told you never to touch my car! You'll mess it up."

A tall man with gray hair—basically, an older version of Brian—stormed over to us. He grabbed

Brian by the elbow and yanked him away from the car. "I'm not going to tell you this again," he said through clenched teeth. "Next time you'll really be sorry."

"Sorry, Dad," said Brian, as his face turned bright red. He really looked terrified. "I was just showing the car to my friends Frank and Joe Hardy. They're here from Bayport."

Friends? Did Brian Conrad actually call us friends? This trip was getting weirder by the minute.

Brian's dad grunted a hello but otherwise ignored us. "Just stay out of trouble," he said to Brian before walking away again. "If you screw up the sale of this car, you're really going to get it."

"I said I was sorry," Brian said in a wavering voice.

Frank looked at me with raised eyebrows. I knew exactly what he was thinking. "Uh, we need to get going," I said.

"Yeah, you really should scram," said Brian. Now that his dad was gone he was suddenly tough again. "You guys don't belong here, anyway. If you knew anything about cars, you wouldn't be tooling around on your dumb little bikes."

"What's wrong with our motorcycles?" I asked.

Frank pulled me away. "It's not worth it," he said. "Let's go. Mom and Dad are waiting."

"Listen to your brother, Joe. I could mess you up so easily," Brian said.

"Whatever," I replied, as Frank and I left the parking lot.

We weren't completely lying about the croquet. Between Tanner's threat, Beller's security guard, and the ominous phone call, one thing was clear: Too many people were suspicious of us. We had to start acting like normal tourists. And apparently, at this place, croquet was something that normal tourists played.

We were thinking strategically, too. We chose croquet because the courts were close to the spa. Picking up some mallets and balls, we headed over to play.

Although I'd heard of the game, I didn't actually know the rules. Turns out Frank didn't have a clue either. We stared out at the courts. They were grassy and filled with white metal squares. They looked like miniature football goalposts, turned upside-down. We started hitting balls through. Simple enough.

"So what do you think?" I asked. "It's got to be Beller, right?"

"Maybe," said Frank. "We know he couldn't stand Henry, but murdering someone on your wedding day seems a little extreme. Did he hate him that much? It's hard to imagine."

"But he didn't do it himself. He just ordered someone else to take care of the whole Operation Bobo thing, right?"

"Yup," Frank replied. "I just wish we knew what that stood for. If it has anything to do with the bomb, that is."

"How could it not?" I asked.

"Who knows?" said Frank. "We could be way off. Maybe Henry was trying to get back at Beller by destroying part of the resort. It's possible that he planted the bomb in one of his cars to throw everyone off, and then accidentally blew himself up."

"If that were the case, he'd have picked any other car. No way would Henry blow up the Duesenberg," I said. "He compared it to a work of art. He loved that car."

"You're sure he wouldn't even do it to frame Beller?" Frank asked.

I shook my head. "There's no way. I'm positive."

"Hey, can I play?"

I turned around. Ashley, the cousin of Ella's

we'd met by the pool, was behind us, holding a croquet mallet. I wondered how much she'd heard.

Frank and I looked at each other. I thought we'd silently come to an agreement, but I said, "Yes," just as Frank was saying, "No."

"Oh, come on, Frank," I said.

Ashley laughed. "Maybe you guys want to discuss this amongst yourselves?" she teased. "I could give you some privacy."

"That's okay," I said. "What my brother means is, of course you can play. It's just that we don't really know what we're doing, so it may be boring for you."

"That's okay," said Ashley. "I can teach you."

Frank glared at me. He clearly thought this was a bad idea. Too bad for him, though. Ashley was too cute to blow off.

"That sounds great, Ashley," I said, handing her my mallet and flashing my brightest smile.

"So, you guys were just talking about the explosion, right?" She shuddered. "What kind of crazy person would do something like that? It makes me nervous, just being here."

"Yeah, it's bad," Frank said. "We were thinking of going home early. In fact, we're supposed to meet our parents in a little while. They're discussing it now."

"Which building are your rooms in?" asked Ashley.

My mind went blank. I looked toward Frank, who turned to Ashley. "We're over by the orchid garden."

"In the C block, you mean?" she asked.

"Yup." We both nodded.

Ashley grinned as she bent over the mallet and stepped on one of the croquet balls. "Did you guys hear the explosion?" she asked, swinging her mallet and knocking a ball through one of the little goalposts.

For some reason, I felt the hair on the back of my neck stand up. I must have still been feeling weird over Henry's death. "We sure did. It was pretty gruesome, huh?"

"The worst," said Ashley. "And I heard there's going to be another one. I figured they'd be warning all the guests by now. You know, so they could evacuate in time."

"How did you hear about the bomb threat?" asked Frank.

"Well, I—"

The rest of Ashley's sentence was drowned out

by gunshots. Soon after that we heard shouting, and then the sounds of a car peeling out.

Suddenly I saw a black Corvette Roadster race by. In the driver's seat was none other than Justin Jones, the M&P car handler.

And he was getting away.

10

The Chase

Justin was on a rampage. He sped across one of the tennis courts, ripping through the net and giving four people in tennis whites the scare of their lives. Veering to the right, he almost took out a golfer, but luckily, the old guy got out of the way just in time.

Joe started running after the car, but I stopped him. "Hold on. He's totally panicked."

"Come on," said Joe, brushing my hand from his arm.

I shook my head. "He doesn't know where he's going, and you don't want to get in his way. It's too dangerous. I'm surprised he hasn't run anyone over yet."

"So what are we supposed to do?" my brother asked.

"Wait for him to self-destruct," I replied.

Wait is not a word my brother likes to hear, but for once he listened to me.

It was a good thing, too. Because moments later we heard sirens in the distance, getting louder and louder.

As we neared the car, we saw Justin driving in circles, because huge trucks blocked most of the paths out. Cop cars were closing in from every direction. Justin had nowhere else to go. Not until one of the trucks happened to pull away, leaving a gaping hole that led straight to the exit. Justin sped toward the open path. It looked like he was going to get away. But in the nick of time, two police cars pulled in front of the Corvette, forcing it to a screeching halt.

Justin was trapped, but he didn't seem to know it—or at least, he wasn't willing to accept it. Basic physics would have told him it was impossible to get around the roadblock. I guess Justin didn't know much basic physics, though, because he sped up and turned sharply.

He crashed straight into the back of one of the cars. The Corvette crumpled like an accordion, and it started smoking almost immediately. The windshield cracked into a spiderweb pattern where Justin hit his head.

We raced to the car, but Justin was out of there before we could stop him. He doubled back across the croquet courts and sprinted past the lap pool.

At least now we were on equal footing. Joe and I were only ten feet behind him when he made it to one of the largest buildings. Chief Malrova and some of his police officers were coming at him on either side. He was cornered.

Or so we thought.

Justin darted inside the building. And by the time Joe and I got there, he'd locked the door behind him.

"Now what?" asked Joe.

Chief Malrova ran up and said, "This door and all of the windows are secure. He's not getting out of there. All we have to do is wait."

Waiting sounded like a horrible idea. Who knew how long he'd try and stay in there? I was counting on Justin to have information about the second bomb. And what if this entire theft was set up to distract us from the real crime?

"With all due respect, chief," I said, "we're running out of time. I think we should go in after him."

Chief Malrova looked from me to the locked-down building. "You boys know what you're doing?" he asked.

Joe and I nodded.

"All right," said the chief. "Go ahead."

Joe didn't think twice before pulling off the screen of a nearby window. Struggling to pry open the glass, he said, "No dice. It's locked."

"Stand back, everyone," I called. Shielding my eyes with my forearm, I kicked a hole in the glass with the heel of my shoe. It shattered loudly. Pieces flew everywhere. I ripped my shirt off and wrapped it around my hand up to my elbow. Reaching inside, I unlocked the window.

After I pulled it open, Joe and I carefully slipped through. We landed on our feet, crunching shards of glass into the plush red carpet. Other than that, the room was silent.

"Now what?" whispered Joe.

I shrugged. We were in some sort of fancy ballroom, and it was a cluttered mess. A tower of crystal champagne glasses balanced in the center of the room. A large chocolate fountain gurgled in one corner. There was a huge, multitiered wedding cake by the stage, and a bunch of large round tables. Each one was draped with a floor-length tablecloth and was decorated with centerpieces of glass and flowers.

There were hiding places everywhere, and no sign of Justin. "He could be under any of these tables," I whispered as we carefully crept around the room.

"So this is where Beller and Ella are getting married," Joe said. He looked around. "I still think a million bucks is way too much to spend on all this crap." He picked a flower out of a nearby centerpiece, sniffed it, and scrunched up his nose. "Blech."

"Shh." I raised a finger to my lips and then held my breath, straining to listen. There was some sort of rustling noise coming from underneath the table by the stage.

Joe and I locked eyes and nodded. This had to be Justin. I tiptoed over and lifted up the tablecloth.

Suddenly a small, white, furry creature shot out the other end.

"What is that thing?" Joe yelled as he jumped backward.

"It's just a dog," I said.

We both stared at the animal. It was barking up a storm and darting between the stage and me and Joe.

"I know that, but where'd it come from?" Joe asked.

I shrugged. "How should I know?"

Joe was just crouching down to pet it when we heard something at the other end of the room. Justin.

He was about to get away. Again.

That's when we noticed the service entrance at the back of the room. Justin was trying to pull the door open, but it was bolted into the floor. He worked the lock open quickly, but we were faster. I made it to Justin first and pounced on him. He went crashing to the floor.

"Dude, get off me!"

"As if," I said through clenched teeth. "Why were you trying to steal the car?"

Justin glared up at me. "What do you care?"

"Why do I care?" I asked. "Oh, I don't know. Maybe I care because I don't want to see hundreds of people die."

Suddenly Justin pulled on the leg of a nearby table, tipping it over so that it came crashing down across my back.

Broken glass—and a broken table—aren't comfy.

I was in so much pain that I couldn't help but loosen my grip, and Justin managed to squirm away. He scrambled across the room, overturning chairs as he went to block our path.

Joe cornered him by the champagne table, but Justin wasn't gonna quit. He upended the whole thing. All the crystal glasses and chilling champagne went sliding off, crashing loudly and falling right at Joe's feet.

"Ouch!" Joe shouted, hunching over and cradling his right leg. "Darn it!"

"Are you okay?" I called.

"Yes," Joe said in a pained voice.

Now I *really* wanted to get this guy.

I cut Justin off by the stage, but he slipped past me. Still, I was so close. The only thing separating us was the table with the enormous wedding cake. I ran around it, but before I caught up with Justin, he lifted the table.

"You wouldn't," I said.

Justin grinned mischievously. Then he lifted the table higher, and the entire cake slipped off and landed on top of me. Suddenly I was covered in white buttercream frosting and knee-deep in sponge cake.

Joe had recovered enough to chase after Justin, but the guy was fast. It didn't help that the little dog kept yipping and jumping, like this was all some sort of game we were playing.

She (I assumed, from her pink collar) kept getting under our feet, and there was no way I was going to kick a defenseless little dog—not even if it had an annoying, high-pitched bark.

Justin shoved Joe and he landed in the chocolate fountain. The dog leaped into Joe's lap.

Justin made his way to the service entrance again. I guess he figured the cops had overlooked that one too—and who knows, maybe he was right.

I had to stop him. Problem was, I was at the other end of the room. I knew that if I tried to run, I wouldn't make it. I had to think of something. Looking around frantically, it suddenly came to me.

I hopped onto the stage, took a running jump, and flew through the air, reaching for the giant disco ball that was hanging from the ceiling.

Bingo. I was on.

Using my momentum, I swung across the room, straight toward Justin. I pulled my legs back and then kicked as hard as I could. *Bam!*

Justin went down, but I knew it wasn't over— and I wasn't going to make the same mistake twice. I let go and landed on top of him. I pushed him onto his stomach and grabbed his hands, holding them firmly behind his back and keeping my knee pressed between his shoulder blades.

"You're not going anywhere," I said. "So you may as well tell us where it is."

"Where *what* is?" asked Justin, spitting blood from his mouth.

"The bomb," I said.

"What are you talking about?" asked Justin.

"Come on, Justin," I said.

"I'm not Justin," he replied.

Okay, whatever. Obviously he wasn't being very cooperative. I signaled to Joe, who'd climbed out of the chocolate fountain and had the dog tucked under his arm.

He quickly unlocked the front doors and ten officers streamed inside the room. So did Henry's security team and the remaining car handlers. Tanner, Maria, Douglas, and . . . wait a minute.

Justin?

I looked at the guy on the floor—the one the cops were now handcuffing and yanking to his feet. He was a Justin lookalike. He had the same freckled face, the same dark curly hair, and he was wearing the same thing: the M&P auction shirt with a pair of khakis.

Yet Justin was standing in front of me. Come to think of it, he was looking really angry, too.

"What's going on?" I asked.

"Jeremy, I can't believe you did this," said Justin. "Officers, this is my twin brother, and I *swear* I had nothing to do with this. Tell them, Jeremy."

"It's true," Jeremy said. "My brother is a goody-goody, much to my disappointment. He refused to help me, which is why I got caught."

Justin was really fuming now. "Don't blame me for this," he yelled. "I'm not the one who's been in and out of juvie since age ten."

"Dude, relax," said Jeremy. "They can't do anything to you. You knew nothing about this."

Justin shook his head. "Of all the stuff to steal, you had to go after something at the M&P auction? This is the best job I've ever had. Thanks for ruining it for me."

Maynard stepped over the mess and walked toward Justin. Putting a hand on his shoulder, he said, "Henry wouldn't want you fired over this. And if I have anything to say about it, whoever takes over the M&P auction house won't let you go either."

"Hey, is that my shirt?" asked Tanner.

Jeremy nodded. "I stole it so I'd be able to blend in. I needed better access to the cars."

"You mean this was all about stealing a car?" I asked.

"Of course," said Jeremy.

"And you have no other motive?"

"What do you mean?" asked Jeremy.

"Yeah, Hardy. What the heck are you talking about?" asked Tanner as he sneered at me. Even Maria looked at me like I was crazy.

I was hugely disappointed. Obviously, Jeremy was just a small-time crook. The guy had nothing to do with the bomb.

Joe and I had to find out who did, though, before it was too late.

As I cleaned the frosting off my chest, I tried to look on the bright side. At least the dog had stopped barking. She was too busy eating the cake that was stuck in my shoelaces. "Will you get this thing away from me?" I asked.

Joe picked up the dog and looked at the tag. "Uh, Frank?" he said.

"Yes?"

"Guess what this dog's name is?"

"Joe, there's no time for this," I said. "We have to find the bomber. I need a new shirt, and you have to get cleaned up too." Looking down at Joe's leg, I noticed it was gushing blood from a cut just below his right knee. I turned to Chief Malrova and asked, "Do you know where we can find a first-aid kit?"

"I'm serious," said Joe. "Guess."

"I don't know," I answered. "Fluffy? Snowflake? Rover?"

Joe shook his head. "It's Bobo."

I raised my eyes to his.

11

Bobo Revealed

Operation Bobo was squirming under my arm. Or at least, Bobo was. It was the weirdest thing. Frank and I checked the dog all over and we didn't see a note, or a sign, or any kind of explosives. As far as we could tell, she was a little ball of white fluff with a bright red collar and a gold name tag. Nothing more.

Still, Chief Malrova was taking every precaution. After we'd patched up my leg and found a new shirt for Frank, he asked us to bring her to the bomb squad so they could check her for explosives. So now we were on our way to the southern tip of the resort. Apparently the squad was waiting in a van marked COMPLETE CATERING.

"Do you think there's a bomb inside her stomach?" I asked. "Like Beller made her swallow something?"

"Could be," said Frank with a shrug. "There's no other feasible explanation."

I shifted Bobo from one arm to the other and said, "I'm surprised Bobo didn't get to the cake before Jeremy did. And as for the chocolate fountain—chocolate's lethal for dogs. It could have killed her."

"Not nearly as lethal as a bomb," Frank pointed out. "Maybe Beller wanted out of his wedding. Blowing up the entire place before the event sure would make a big statement. The ceremony would have to be canceled and he'd get to collect all that insurance money after the resort was destroyed."

"I still think he planned this to get back at Henry," I said.

"Well, he already did that. Or someone already did. So why the second, larger bomb?"

"Maybe Beller didn't know about the Duesenberg when he gave the orders," I said. "Maybe he just needed a temporary hiding place for the dog. Maybe Bobo is supposed to be somewhere else for the three p.m. explosion."

We both walked faster and finally found the bomb squad van parked by the eighteen hole of the golf course. Once we got there, we handed Bobo over to one of the detectives.

"You won't have to harm her, will you?" I asked.

The guy shook his head. "No, we'll just put her through an X-ray machine, and test her skin and saliva for traces of ammonium nitrate and other bomb-making chemicals."

Frank and I waited outside, kicking around the same old theories without coming up with any new ideas. About ten minutes later, the guy handed Bobo back to us. "She's clean," he said.

"Okay." I took the dog, who seemed very happy to see me. I threw my head back so she'd stop licking my face, but she still managed to nail my chin with her small pink tongue.

Frank asked, "Uh, what are we supposed to do with her now?"

The guy shrugged. "Don't know. Not our problem." Then he slammed the door closed and drove off.

"Now what?" I asked.

"Let's go back to the ballroom," said Frank. "Let Chief Malrova deal with Bobo."

We were just passing by the spa when we heard someone scream. "Bobo?"

I turned around and saw Ella Sinclair running toward me. One of Beller's security guards was trailing her by a few feet. Lucky for us, it wasn't the same guard from the spa this morning. I'd be pretty happy if I didn't see that woman ever again.

"You know this dog?" I asked.

Rather than answer me, Ella scooped Bobo out of my arms and started kissing her.

"Bobo, what happened to you? You're such a mess," cried Ella, as she held the dog at arm's length so she could inspect her.

Okay—Frank's jeans were still covered in cake, and I had chocolate coming out of my ears, but Ella was focused only on the dog, who wasn't even *that* dirty.

Huh?

"So Bobo is yours?" Frank asked Ella.

"Yes, she is," said Ella, squeezing the dog, who kept licking her face. "Where did you find her?"

"In the ballroom back there," Frank pointed over his shoulder.

"You mean where I'm getting married?" she asked.

I nodded. "Yes, exactly."

"You're kidding." Ella looked from Frank to me, and back to Frank again. "Wait a minute," she said, pointing down at his jeans. "Is that my wedding cake you're wearing?"

Frank turned bright red. He glanced down at himself and said, "Um, I think so."

Ella's eyes widened. "What happened?" she asked.

"Long story," said Frank.

"I have time," Ella replied.

"Um, someone stole one of the cars from the M&P auction, and he ended up hiding out in the ballroom where you're getting married," I said. "The thief—Jeremy is his name—he got a little destructive."

"How do you mean?" asked Ella.

"Well, he sort of knocked over the cake," said Frank. "And that champagne tower thing, and then some of the tables."

"The chocolate fountain isn't in great shape either," I added. "The good news is, the cops caught the bad guy."

"Okay, but how bad is the ballroom?" Ella wondered.

I looked to Frank, who just shook his head. Turning back to Ella, I said, "Look, it's probably better if we just show you."

As we took off for the room, Frank said, "I'm sure they can fix everything in time."

I didn't agree, but it's not like I was going to say so in front of Ella.

The police had hauled off Jeremy by now. They must have finished their investigation, too, because except for the big fat mess, the ballroom was empty.

Ella gazed around. Her eyes were wide open and disbelieving. She kept opening her mouth to speak, but no words would come. Finally she asked, "Bobo did all of this?"

"Not exactly," I said. "You see, there was this car chase, and then a crash, and the guy escaped. And then we found out he wasn't really who we'd thought and . . ." My voice trailed off when I noticed Ella staring at me with this completely confused expression on her face.

"It's a long story," I said.

Ella didn't say anything for a few moments. I guess she was taking in the mess. The fountain had tipped over, and the chocolate that wasn't on me was now seeping into the red carpet. The broken cake was on the floor. Maybe the top tier could be salvaged, but probably not. A few of the tables were on their sides, and there was glass everywhere.

I thought Ella was going to scream at us. So it was a total surprise when she started laughing.

"What's so funny?" I asked.

Ella's face was bright red, and she was gasping for air. She was too hysterical to even answer me.

"Why are you laughing? This is a very bad situation. You're supposed to get married here in just a few hours, and this place is in shambles." Something about Ella's laugh was infectious, though.

Even as I said it, I started cracking up. Frank did too.

"This is *not* a laughing matter," my brother said, between gales of laughter.

"I can't help it," she said. "It's just that Jake hates this dog. He begged me not to bring her to Phoenix. I finally had to sneak her in here, and he was so mad when he found out. So it's funny that Bobo was involved, and . . ."

Ella's voice trailed off. Her eyes narrowed. "Jake," she whispered. "I don't believe it. How could he?"

She wasn't laughing anymore.

Neither were we. I looked to Frank, who shrugged. We had no idea what she was talking about.

Ella went to the door and screamed, "Jake Beller!"

Her security guard rushed forward and asked, "Is there something wrong, ma'am?"

"There sure is," she said, her voice hardened to a tone that was all business. "Get me Jake, please."

The guy said something into his walkie-talkie, and a few minutes later, Beller came rushing over to the ballroom.

"What's the problem, sweetheart?" Beller asked. He seemed really worried about Ella, but when he realized the room was destroyed, he got furious. "What happened here? Who did this? I want to know who did this. Someone's going to pay for this! Don't worry, baby. It can all be fixed. We'll fly in another cake, and there's plenty more crystal. . . ."

"Stop it," said Ella. "I don't care about the stupid room. I don't care about the cake or the crystal or anything. What I care about is Bobo." She held the dog up to Beller's face. Bobo growled and bared her teeth at him.

"Get that thing away from me," said Beller, taking a few steps back and putting his hand in front of his face. "You know I'm deathly allergic to dogs."

"You can't be allergic to Bobo," said Ella. "She's a hypoallergenic dog. She's got hair instead of fur, so she doesn't shed."

"You've told me that a million times," said Beller. "That doesn't change the fact that she gives me hives."

"So your solution is to kidnap her on our wedding day?" Ella screamed. "How could you?"

Frank and I walked a few feet away so we could figure out our next move without being heard. Not that they'd bother listening to us. Beller and Ella were wrapped up in their argument. The security guard just stood there, not saying a word, but watching them both like spectators at a tennis match.

"Beller still may be guilty in all this," I said.

"Good point," Frank replied. "We'd better call for backup." Flipping open his phone, he called Chief Malrova and asked him to hurry to the ballroom. Then we walked back over to the not-so-happy couple, to make sure Beller would stay where he was.

Beller was now shouting to be heard over Bobo's barks. "You promised me you'd leave her at home. Remember, I hired that veterinarian to take care of her because you didn't want her staying with just any dog sitter?"

"Bobo can't miss my wedding day," said Ella. "I've known her longer than I've known you."

Beller shook his head angrily. "You've known everyone longer than you've known me. We just met two months ago."

"That's not the point," said Ella.

"Look," said Beller. "The plan was just to keep her away until tomorrow. That was it. I promise. After that, I'd figure something else out."

"The *plan*?" Ella screamed. "There was a plan?"

"Operation Bobo," I said. Everything started coming together. Turning to Beller, I asked, "So the phone call you made at the spa was to the dognapper?"

"What?!" Ella shrieked.

"There is no dognapper," Beller insisted, turning quickly to Ella. "Will you relax?"

"No!" Ella shouted. "I won't. Not until you explain yourself."

Beller turned to the security guard. "The call was to you. Now, what went wrong?"

"The dog is vicious," the guard said sheepishly. "She bit me. Broke the skin and everything. I realized I needed backup, but I wanted to make sure she was safe, so I stashed her in here. She was only supposed to be in the ballroom for a few minutes, but then suddenly there were police surrounding the place, and I figured I'd better scram. I came back to warn you, but you were still having the massage."

"You're fired!" Beller yelled at the guard. "You've ruined the entire wedding."

"Don't you dare fire him," said Ella. "You're the one who ruined the wedding. This is all your fault, Jake."

Just then Chief Malrova showed up. "There you are," he said, hurrying into the ballroom. "So I here there's no bomb in Bobo?"

"She's clean," I said.

"We're still not sure about Beller, though," Frank added.

"Wait, what are you talking about? Why would there be a bomb in the dog?" asked Beller. "You

116

don't think that I'm the crazy person who's been threatening to blow this place up?"

"You're crazy enough to kidnap your fiancée's dog," I pointed out.

"That's different," said Beller. "She's just a dog. Why would I blow up my own hotel?"

"You said Henry Peterson would pay. You said this would be his last auction ever, and now he's dead!" I shouted.

Beller narrowed his eyes at me. "You should be more careful about making accusations like that," he said. "You don't know what you're talking about. And besides, who are you, coming in here and announcing I'm a suspect?"

"I know you said those things," I replied. "Frank heard them too."

My brother nodded.

"I'm not denying that I said them," said Beller. "But you're taking this all out of context. The reason I said that Henry would pay is because I was about to buy his auction house out from under him."

"What?" I asked.

"It's a publicly traded corporation," Beller explained. "And I just became the majority shareholder. If Henry had lived, he'd be working for me. Until I fired him, that is."

"Prove it," said Frank.

"I don't need to prove anything to you kids," said Beller.

Chief Malrova stepped up. "Actually Beller, you do. Frank and Joe aren't your average kids. They're connected to some of the country's most powerful law enforcement agents. Plus, they're working very hard to ensure the safety of you and your guests this weekend. So you'd better show some respect."

Beller cocked an eyebrow. "Fine," he replied. He got on the phone with his lawyer and asked him to rush over the paperwork.

"Now, if you don't mind," said Beller, snapping his phone shut, "I would like to get back to planning my wedding."

Ella laughed. "That's what you think," she said.

Clearly exasperated, Beller threw his hands up and asked, "What's the problem *now*?"

"There's not going to be any wedding, Jake," Ella replied. "Bobo and I are going home." Turning on her heel, she walked away without a single glance back.

"Wait a second," said Beller as he ran after Ella and Bobo. The security guard followed.

"I'll handle this, boys," said Chief Malrova, as he chased after them.

Once Frank and I were left alone, he said to me, "This is totally nuts."

I shook my head, trying to make sense of all the craziness. We'd foiled an evil twin and a dog-napping fiancé, but we still hadn't cracked the real case.

And then Frank's phone rang. As soon as he answered it, his face went pale.

"It's the bomber?" I whispered.

Frank nodded.

12

Busted

"Yes?" I said into the phone.

"Pretty gnarly chase scene, don't you think?" asked the same muffled voice from earlier.

"Who is this?" I demanded.

"I'm not telling," he replied.

The guy was really getting on my nerves. "It's one o'clock. You've had your fun. People are going to die unless you tell me where you hid the bomb."

"Don't worry," the guy replied. "You'll find out soon enough."

"But—"

Click. The phone went dead.

I flipped it over and zoomed in on the map.

Little did the guy know that, thanks to my tracer, "soon enough" was actually right about now.

"Do you have the location?" asked Joe, as we both huddled over the tracer. I held my phone so tightly that my knuckles turned white.

The next few seconds seemed like an eternity, but finally we saw the blinking red light. The caller was back at the car auction.

"I'll bet it's Tanner," I said as we raced to the scene. "Maynard's excuse that he was jealous of me and Maria was a little too convenient. Come to think of it, maybe they're working together."

I glanced at my brother, who was just a couple of steps behind me. His leg was bleeding through the bandage. "Does that hurt?" I asked.

"Nah," said Joe. "I'm fine."

I knew he was bluffing, but there wasn't time to argue. Joe wasn't about to let his injury get in the way of our mission, and I didn't blame him. I just hoped it would all be over soon, for his sake *and* for the sake of the hundreds of Billington Resort guests.

Because honestly? I was starting to freak out. Never had I seen the kind of devastation we might witness if we failed.

Fortunately, we didn't fail often. And I was determined not to this time.

When we finally got to the auction, we found it plenty crowded. There were three times as many people in the parking lot since we'd last been there, and an excited energy filled the air. It looked like the selling had already begun. All the cars were lined up and ready to go. Maria was sitting in the silver Cadillac, and the car was perched on the auction block.

This British dude was in charge of the bidding. When he called out numbers, he spoke so quickly that all of his words ran together. "We have $100,000. Do I hear $125,000? Come on, 125. Someone? Beautiful car. Mint condition. Going once, going twice. Yes, thank you, gentleman in the back with the green shirt. $125,000. I have 125. 125. Now do I hear $150,000?"

Tanner was shining a blue Jaguar. When he saw me and Joe approach, he smirked. This guy had such an attitude—too much to be totally innocent.

I checked the scanner. No dice. The red light was still moving, and in fact, the bomber was heading toward one end of the parking lot, near the exit. We had to hurry.

I headed to the left, and Joe followed close behind.

A minute later we zoomed in on the bomber.

The guy was wearing a black baggy sweatshirt. The hood was pulled up around his face, so there was no way we'd be able to recognize him.

It looked like he was on the phone, but as soon as he saw us approach, he ran.

"Stop," I yelled, as if he would actually listen to me. "Get back here!"

He was heading toward the other end of the parking lot.

We chased him, but before we got close enough to ID him, he threw himself into his car—a beat-up silver hybrid.

As he sped away I realized that now Joe and I were really stuck. There wasn't a cop car in sight. Where was everyone?

"Too bad we left our bikes behind," Joe said.

I turned around and looked at the long line of shiny sports cars behind us. "Well, we do have the next best thing."

"Huh?" asked Joe.

"Follow me," I said. I ran to the end of the line and opened up the door to the first convertible I saw. It just happened to be Brian Conrad's dad's BMW 507. And, by some stroke of luck, the keys were inside.

"Really?" asked Joe.

"I hate to do this, but it's for a good cause," I said as I got in and gunned the engine. "Why don't you take a different one? I'm hoping we can cut him off."

Joe didn't need to be asked twice. He ran past a few cars and hopped into the green Aston Martin. "I've been wanting to drive one of these ever since I saw my first James Bond movie," he shouted. "Let's get this sleazeball."

We revved up our engines and started to pull away. We didn't make it very far, though, because Maynard jumped in front of our path and drew his gun.

I screeched to a stop. "You move another inch and I'm shooting," said Maynard.

My jaw locked as I stared down the barrel of the gun. I wanted to argue, but for some reason I couldn't find my voice.

Joe started honking the horn. He leaned his head out the car window and yelled, "Dude, don't shoot. We've got to go. Just trust us. This is an emergency."

When I finally snapped out of it, I started pleading with the guy too. "Seriously, Maynard. We'll explain everything to you later."

"I thought there was something strange about you two," Maynard said. He was clearly not willing to budge. "You guys asked too many questions. I should have known you had an ulterior motive. First Justin's twin, and now you—if Henry were around to see this, he wouldn't believe it."

Chief Malrova raced over. "Are you going after the bomber?" he asked me.

"We sure are," I said. "He took off a few minutes ago, but we can still catch him. If we can get out of here, that is."

Malrova flashed his badge at Maynard. "I order you to let the boys borrow these cars."

"Okay," said Maynard, lowering his gun. "I'm not going to argue with the cops." He stepped out of our path, and we sped away.

We didn't have any trouble finding the bomber. The resort exit let out onto a one-way street, and the guy was stalled at a light, just half a mile away. But when he saw us approach, he sped through it, narrowly missing getting hit by a truck. As soon as it was safe, Joe and I ran the light too.

We followed the bomber as he pulled onto the freeway. Soon we were all weaving in and out of cars.

I stared at my speed gauge, watching as it quickly went from seventy, to eighty, to ninety, and even a hundred.

The bomber quickly turned off the freeway. Joe

and I did the same. We were speeding down a sub-
urban street at close to a hundred miles an hour.
And the Toyota was no match for the sports cars.
We were practically on his tail.

The desert sun beat down intensely, but the guy
was still wearing his hood so I couldn't ID him.

Suddenly he veered off into the dirt.

I didn't know how these old cars would handle
on the desert landscape, but I was about to find
out. Yanking the steering wheel to the right, I followed.

It was a bumpy, bone-rattling ride as I sped past
cacti and boulders and tumbleweed. The suburban
sprawl of Phoenix faded behind us. We were heading into nowhere. Miles and miles of desert
stretched out before me.

And I was so close to the bomber—that is, until
my car started shaking even more violently than
before. Next, I started seeing things kind of fuzzy. I
blinked, not knowing what was up. Smoke was ris-
ing from the hood of the car, and the dials on the
dashboard were spinning like crazy. Something was
seriously wrong with the BMW.

The car made a clanking, growling noise and
then petered out to a stop.

It must have overheated.

As Joe sped past me, he turned his head and yelled, "You okay?" He started slowing down.

"It's just the car, but forget about me," I shouted. "Go after the bomber!"

Suddenly Joe's car made a huge arc through the desert. A thin layer of dust rose up into the air. He was coming back for me.

We didn't have any time to spare, so I climbed to the hood of my car.

Joe whipped by me and then pulled a fast 180. Soon he was racing toward me.

When he was just a few feet away, I leaped from the hood of the BMW and landed in the Aston Martin.

I guess he was going faster than I realized, because I ended up in the backseat.

"Nice move," Joe called over his shoulder.

"Always works in the movies," I said, as I quickly scrambled to the front seat of the car. "Let's get this guy."

Joe shifted the car into third, fourth, and then fifth gear. Within moments we were right on the tail of the Toyota.

The bomber veered left, catching us by surprise and throwing us off track. Suddenly he had the lead again.

This chase could go on for hours. The desert was huge and sprawling. There were mountains in the distance, but for all I knew, they were hundreds of miles away. We were running out of time.

Not good.

Suddenly we heard a loud popping noise, and the Toyota slowed to a crawl.

The guy had a flat! He stopped the car, leaped out, and made a run for it.

Joe slammed on the brakes and we scrambled out.

When I finally got close enough, I grabbed him. Joe pulled back his hood. I couldn't believe my eyes.

The person who was making the threatening phone calls? The one who was responsible for the bomb that was going to wipe the Billington Resort clear off the map?

Ashley McGill.

SUSPECT PROFILE

<u>Name:</u> Ashley McGill

<u>Hometown:</u> Riverside, California

<u>Physical description:</u> 19 years old, 5'9", blond hair, blue eyes.

<u>Occupation:</u> College student in Wisconsin

<u>Background:</u> Has lived all over, everywhere from Florida to France, Tokyo to Colorado.

<u>Suspicious behavior:</u> She knew too much about the bomb for a regular wedding guest. She was always popping up at inconvenient times.

<u>Suspected of:</u> Killing Henry Peterson with a car bomb and planting a second bomb that may blow up the Billington Resort.

<u>Possible motives:</u> It can't be just to get out of going to a boring wedding, so she must have some other problem with Beller.

13

Too Little, Too Late

I was so stunned to find out the truth, I loosened my grip. She kicked me in the shins, elbowed Frank in his stomach, and then broke free.

Frank and I started our chase after Ashley. It was the same desert scene, but now we were on foot. "Of all the suspects on our list, I can't believe it didn't occur to us to add Ashley McGill."

"It should have been obvious from the start," said Frank. "She kept popping up at the most inconvenient times. Plus, she's got some major beef against Beller's environmental policies."

"True," I said. "Though she probably wouldn't use that terminology."

"Huh?" asked Frank.

"If she's so militant about the environment, I'll bet she's a vegetarian, too," I replied.

We were both sprinting now. Ashley was so close. I reached out to grab her, but she shot forward.

Frank lunged, but missed her by a hair.

Moments later she stumbled on a rock and we caught up to her. I managed to get her in a head-lock. Frank pulled her hands behind her back and slapped on the handcuffs we'd borrowed from Chief Malrova earlier in the day.

"Let me go," Ashley cried, as she struggled to pull free.

"Now why would we do that?" I asked.

"Because Beller is the real criminal here," said Ashley.

"You mean he planted the bomb?" Frank asked. "Now I'm really confused."

"No," Ashley replied. "I planted the bomb, but only because Beller is destroying the environment. He needs to be taught a lesson."

Oh boy, I thought. *What a whack job.* "You really believe that, don't you?"

"Of course," she said.

Frank loaded Ashley into the back of the Aston Martin and then slid inside after her. "You need to tell us where the bomb is," he said. "This is important."

"I'm not talking," said Ashley.

"You're already responsible for one death. Do you really want to have hundreds more on your conscience?" asked Frank.

"Jake Beller is the one who should be worried about his conscience," said Ashley. "He's been buying up all this beautiful desert land in the name of corporate profits. Do you know how much wildlife he's killed with his construction projects? Eagles have been displaced. Snakes have been run over by tractors. There are bats and jackrabbits and all sorts of insects that he's ignoring. More than a quarter of our country's frogs and toads live in Arizona, but do you think Beller cares?"

"This is unbelievable," I said, putting the car into gear and heading for the highway. "We're talking about human beings here. How is killing Henry Peterson saving the animals?"

"The first bomb was supposed to be a warning," said Ashley. "Henry wasn't supposed to be in the car."

"Try telling that to Henry," said Frank. "Oh wait, you can't—because you've already killed him!"

"You guys are failing to see the bigger picture here," said Ashley.

What a lunatic! I glared at her in the rearview

mirror. The more she tried to explain herself, the angrier I got.

"It was supposed to be symbolic," Ashley explained. "Those muscle cars use so much gas with their V-eight engines. They destroy the environment. It's the same mentality. But like I said before, Henry wasn't supposed to die. He shouldn't have even been inside that car. They gave me his schedule. He was supposed to be in a meeting with hotel management at the other end of the resort. I didn't mean to hurt anyone."

"He loved that car," I said.

"It's a sad thing to love a machine," said Ashley.

"Don't go moralizing on me," I said. "You're responsible for a man's death."

"And hundreds more, too, if you don't tell us where the bomb is," Frank added.

"Stop trying to scare me," said Ashley. "I'm not falling for it. I know they'll evacuate the resort. And then Beller's wedding will be ruined. He doesn't deserve any better. Trust me."

"Ashley, you don't understand. They're not evacuating. No one believes the bomb is real," I insisted.

"You're bluffing," said Ashley. "If I told you now, all I'd be saving is a bunch of horrible buildings. Buildings that never should have been there in the first place."

I checked my watch. It was already 2:00 p.m. and we'd barely made it to the freeway. Ashley obviously wasn't able to realize the truth. We'd have to prove it to her. I stepped on the gas and leaned forward. *Come on, car,* I silently pleaded. *Don't fail me now.*

"Who are you working for?" asked Frank.

"No one," Ashley replied. She bit her bottom lip and glanced out the window.

"You said 'they' gave you Henry's schedule," Frank pointed out. "We know you're not alone in this, and at some point, we're going to find out who your partner or manager is—so you may as well tell us now."

Ashley shook her head. Frank and I continued questioning her, but she didn't say another word for the entire drive.

Fifteen minutes later we were at the resort. The auction was still going strong. They'd sold about half the cars, and the buyers were bidding on an antique Porsche. We got out of the car and wove in and out of the crowd in search of Chief Malrova. When we finally found him, we handed Ashley over.

"She's part of some environmental terrorist group," Frank explained. "But she won't tell us which one."

"And she won't tell us where the bomb is," I added.

Ashley blinked at the crowd. "What's everyone doing here?" she asked. "Aren't they scared?"

I shook my head sadly. "I told you, Ashley. No one believes the bomb threat is real."

Chief Malrova looked Ashley in the eye. "Look at all these people, Ashley. Even if we started evacuating now, we won't get very far. Some of them are going to die, unless you cooperate."

Ashley peered out at the crowd in disbelief. Her face went pale and her hands were shaking. "I don't believe it," she said. "You guys were right. And now it's too late."

14

The Awful Truth

"It's not too late," I said. "Tell us where it is."

Ashley's eyes welled up with tears.

"If you tell us now," said Chief Malrova, "things will be easier for you later."

"It's two thirty-eight," Joe reminded her. "Twenty-two minutes to go. Are you really willing to live with all these deaths on your hands?"

"She won't have to live with it," I said. "She'll die too. We all will."

"It's in the ballroom where Beller and Ella are getting married," Ashley blurted out. "In the disco ball that's hanging over the dance floor."

Chief Malrova grabbed his walkie-talkie and ordered the bomb squad to the ballroom. He left Ashley with some other officers.

Then the three of us ran to the site.

By the time we got to the building, the Complete Catering truck was already parked out front. The same guys who'd checked out Bobo were now on the case.

As I watched them lower the disco ball from the ceiling and crack it open, my stomach got queasy and my knees felt weak. All I could think about was how, just a few hours earlier, I was hanging from that very same disco ball when I went after Jeremy. If it had fallen under my weight, it would have tripped the bomb and we would have died instantly.

Joe put his hand on my shoulder. "Kind of a close call, huh?"

"That's an understatement if I ever heard one," I replied. I checked my watch. It was 2:45.

The next fifteen minutes were the slowest fifteen minutes of my life. The wires connecting the explosives were tied in knots and secured with putty. The team had to work very carefully to disassemble everything. Of course, they also had to work quickly. They had no time to spare.

It came down to the last few seconds, but finally the bomb squad succeeded in defusing the bomb.

Once everything was safe, we followed Chief Malrova back to the parking lot so we could question Ashley.

"You have to tell us who you're working for," I said. "This was too close of a call. Can you imagine what would have happened if we didn't find you in time?"

"Yes, I'd be back in college and everything would be fine," said Ashley.

"Fine for you, but not for the hundreds of guests you murdered," said Joe.

"No one was supposed to be here," said Ashley. "This is Beller's fault."

"I don't think the judge is going to see it that way," said Chief Malrova. "We'll give you one last chance. You're going to prison anyway, but trust me. They're not too kind to terrorists who refuse to cooperate."

"They promised me no one would get hurt. Everything was supposed to be so simple," Ashley said.

"Who are 'they'?" I asked.

After a long pause Ashley sighed deeply and said, "Ecology First."

"I should have known," said Chief Malrova. "Ecology First is the most aggressive environmental terrorist group out there."

He didn't have to tell me. I knew all about them. They were infamous for using extreme measures to get their statement across. And their leaders were wanted for crimes in at least three states.

"Isn't that the group that spiked all those trees in Oregon, causing the deaths of five loggers?" asked Joe.

Chief Malrova nodded. "Sure is. They also blew up commercial fishing vessels off the coast of California, killing about twenty."

"That's only because the nets they used to capture fish also killed seals," said Ashley.

"Look," I said. "I'm all for protecting the environment, but only through legal channels."

"People need a wake-up call," said Ashley.

"You may be right," I said. "But you're not going to win any supporters like this."

Chief Malrova loaded Ashley into the back of a police car and sent her away.

As the police sirens faded, he turned to us and said, "Interesting priorities!"

"I'm not agreeing with her methods, but she's right about this resort being pretty wasteful," I said.

"Well, you can tell that to Beller yourself," said the chief. "He's asked to meet with you boys."

"We'd better do it fast," I said. "We have a plane to catch."

Chief Malrova led us toward Beller's office at the other end of the resort.

Before we made it through the car auction, though, we heard an angry voice call, "Frank and Joe Hardy—where've you been?"

I turned around to find Brian looking at us with daggers in his eyes. "Oh, hi," I said.

"I saw you guys take off in my dad's car. You're gonna pay for that." He turned to Chief Malrova and said, "These guys are crooks."

"Actually, these boys are heroes," the chief replied. "They used the car to track down a vicious terrorist. If it weren't for them, none of us would be standing here right now."

We weren't expecting medals or anything, but it would have been nice if the chief's explanation had at least stopped Brian from looking like he wanted to strangle us.

"So where's my dad's car?" he asked.

"Somewhere north of here, in the desert," I said. "It overheated."

"We'll call a tow truck," said Chief Malrova. "Don't worry about the car."

"But you should really fix that thing before you try and sell it," Joe added. "It's kind of a shoddy piece of tin, don't you think?"

Brian said, "You guys may have fooled the chief, but you haven't fooled me. You'd better watch your backs."

"Whatever," I said. We both kept on walking.

This seemed to upset him more, but what did we care?

Beller's office was on the third floor above the hotel lobby. It was a large glass box with views of Phoenix and the desert and the mountains beyond.

When we walked in we found Beller sitting behind an enormous desk in a wide leather swivel chair. "Frank and Joe Hardy," he said. "So we meet again."

"Sorry about crashing the spa," I said.

Beller waved his hand as if to brush the idea out of my head. "Oh, that doesn't matter. I know I was wary of you two, but I want to thank you for saving my resort."

"We're just doing our jobs," I said.

"Well, I appreciate it," said Beller. "And I'm glad you're on my side."

"Oh, I wouldn't go that far," I said. "We're on the side of justice. Ashley's methods were pretty extreme, but she raises some good points."

"Yeah," Joe agreed. "Like, do you really need an orchid garden in the desert? And why did you buy all that empty land? Do you really have to build more houses and malls and parking lots? We heard you outbid that environmental group that wanted to turn the land into a national park. That's kind of sleazy."

"That's also none of your business," said Beller.

"True," I said. "But is it really good business

sense to destroy all of the existing nature out here? Don't people come to the desert so they can actually see the desert?"

"Hmm," said Beller. "You may have a point. I suppose I could at least look into setting aside some of that land for a national park."

"It would be nice," I said. "And I think everyone would be better off in the long run."

"We should really get to the airport," said Joe. "It was nice meeting you. And I hope you and Ella enjoy the rest of this beautiful weather."

"We will, I'm sure—but not necessarily together. There's not going to be a wedding. Ella has left me," said Beller.

"Sorry about that, sir," I said, as if it was new news.

"It's okay," said Beller. "Kidnapping her dog was a little extreme—but we had some other unresolvable issues. We were probably rushing into things. Anyway, as a token of my thanks, I'd like to give you boys something."

"We can't accept money," said Joe. "We're just doing our jobs."

"Oh, I wasn't going to offer you any money," said Beller, a slight smile tugging at his lips. He reached under his desk and pulled out two sun visors. Each was blue with bright yellow writing that read, THE BILLINGTON RESORT AND SPA.

Unbelievable.

Joe opened his mouth to protest, but I cut him off. "Thank you, sir. We sure appreciate this." I pulled him out of the office before he let Beller know what he was really thinking.

On our way to the airport, we chucked the visors in the trash. It's not like we weren't grateful. It's just that if Mom found them, we'd have a hard time explaining.

Okay, maybe we were a little ungrateful. Joe was right. Sun visors are lame. Plus, the guy's a billionaire and we just saved his entire resort from being blown away, and after discussing the environmental hazards of his building projects, he offers us something from his gift shop?

I wasn't going to miss the Billington Resort one bit.

15

Getting Even

We were so tired when we got back to Tahoe. Hard to believe that so much happened in a day. It felt like we'd been away for a week. At the same time, it seemed like time had frozen. Everything was so normal. It was the exact same scene as last night. But this time Dad was in the kitchen making dinner, and Mom was relaxing on the sofa in the living room, watching the news.

"Hi, boys," said Mom, looking up from the television. "How was the skiing?"

"It was great," I said.

"You know, I looked for you on the slopes, but I didn't see you once, all day."

"That's strange," Frank said, flopping down in

the easy chair next to her. "We were on the mountain from sunup to sundown."

As I walked to the kitchen to say hi to Dad, Mom stopped me. "Wait a minute, Joe," she said. "Why are you limping?"

I had no choice but to roll up my ski pants. I'd changed into them just before entering the house.

Sneaky, huh?

Once Mom saw my bandaged leg, she asked, "Were you showing off again?"

"He was," Frank cut in, before I could argue. "I tried to stop him too. But there was this girl he was trying to impress, and—well, you know Joe."

I narrowed my eyes at him and whispered, "I'll get you for that."

"Just try," he whispered back.

"Oh, Joe," Mom said.

"I'm fine," I insisted. "It doesn't even hurt."

Mom sighed and said, "I just wish you'd be more careful. Someday you may really hurt yourself." She turned back to the TV.

Just then the newscaster announced a breaking news report. It was about a near-catastrophe at the Billington Resort in Phoenix, Arizona.

Mom said, "The Billington? That sounds so familiar. . . . Isn't that the one owned by Jake Beller?"

"Don't know," I replied, grinning at Frank.

"I think I read he's getting married again," said Mom.

As I watched the television, my eyes widened in horror. There was a shot of the car auction on-screen, and in the background I saw myself and Frank.

I leaped toward the TV and turned it off before Mom spotted us.

"Hey, I was watching the news," Mom said. "Do you mind?"

I smiled at her. "Come on, we're on vacation. Have you seen the mountains outside? How can you think about television when we're in the middle of such natural beauty?"

"Okay," said Mom. "Point taken, which reminds me—I know you boys were listening to Beethoven last night, so I got you something."

Mom rifled through her purse and then handed me some CDs.

I flipped through them. There was some Vivaldi, more Beethoven, and something by this dude named Handel.

"I thought we'd listen to them after dinner. Doesn't that sound like fun?" she asked.

Frank and I locked eyes. There was no way out of this one.

Or was there?

I handed the CDs back to Mom. "Thanks, I'd love to listen to these, but actually, my leg is hurting a lot. I think I'd be better off crashing right after we eat."

"Okay, honey," said Mom. "I guess we can listen some other time."

"No, I'd hate to deny you and Dad and Frank the pleasure. So please, listen without me."

"Are you sure?" asked Mom.

"It's a sacrifice, but hopefully it'll teach me a valuable lesson about being such a show-off," I said.

"Wonderful," Mom said happily.

"Yeah, wonderful," Frank repeated, although he wasn't quite so enthused.

Once Mom went into the kitchen to check on Dad, Frank turned to me and said, "Thanks a lot."

I stretched out on the couch with my hands behind my head and smiled.

CLUE IN TO THE CLASSIC MYSTERIES OF THE HARDY BOYS®
FROM GROSSET & DUNLAP

$6.99 ($9.99 CAN) each

AVAILABLE AT YOUR LOCAL BOOKSTORE OR LIBRARY

Grosset & Dunlap • A division of Penguin Young Readers Group
A member of Penguin Group (USA), Inc. • A Pearson Company
www.penguin.com/youngreaders

THE HARDY BOYS is a trademark of Simon & Schuster, Inc., registered in the United States Patent and Trademark Office.

Exciting fiction from three-time Newbery Honor author Gary Paulsen

Newbery Honor Book

Newbery Honor Book

Aladdin Paperbacks and Simon Pulse
Simon & Schuster Children's Publishing
www.SimonSays.com